PALU

PALU

Louis Nowra

ST. MARTIN'S PRESS
NEW YORK

Library of Congress Cataloging-in-Publication Data

Nowra, Louis, 1950–
    Palu.

    1. Title.
PR9619.3.N64P35   1989   823   88-30573
ISBN 0-312-02626-9

First published in Australia by Pan Books Pty Limited.

First U.S. Edition

10 9 8 7 6 5 4 3 2 1

TO VERONICA KELLY

PALU

SOMETIME IN THE next few days my husband will have me put to death. I have overheard the guards saying that this will not happen, that I will be kept in prison until I die a natural death. No one will have their wife executed, they say. But I know my husband and I know he will carry out his threat; because I am the past and a part of him he wishes to forget. Just as some governments destroy or alter the past by erasing their former leaders from photographs, so my husband wishes to obliterate me.

These words are my race against time and an attempt to set the record straight. If I do not do this then he will belong to only legends and myths and the truth will vanish forever. If the future knows the truth then I will defeat him. Is it any wonder he is scared of me? I know he is because I can feel his dread. At night I sense him in this cell and his spirit is shivering uncontrollably. He moans and curses me with the foulest words he knows; *witch, bloodclot, whore, shit, dog.* His fear is so powerful that my soul is gripped by it. My teeth begin to chatter and my body shake as if in some monstrous sympathy with him. And filling my cell like an evil wind is a whistling, swirling around and around me, making me so terrified that I vomit until my stomach is empty. I live this nightmare until the sun comes up and I can finally sleep, exhausted, my lips dry and cracked with fear.

On such nights as these I am thankful for the guard who comes to make love to me, his mouth smelling of ginger and spicy barks. The touch of another human calms me. Even though he is silent throughout it all, for fear that if he engages me in conversation I will enchant him, I am grateful to feel his harsh hands grabbing me, for at these moments the power of lust takes over and I can forget you, however briefly.

The guard likes to pretend that he is not scared of me but it is partly the reason why he first raped me and visits me whenever he is on duty. The idea of copulating with a witch and the President's wife is such a potent aphrodisiac that he will risk his life to experience it. Because he is an insensitive, clumsy man he does not know that I am using him to ward off my nightmare. It is he who gave me this paper and pencil as payment for keeping quiet about his visits and writing these words has helped comfort me. For I'll tell you straight, I am scared shitless of dying.

I like this guard's breath. I know the ginger and spicy barks are used to keep my spirit from entering his mouth, but the sweet smell is a relief from the stench of death which has impregnated every stone pore of this cell. That is not a rusting wall opposite me; that is the blood of tortured prisoners. Even my cell gecko avoids that wall.

The guard is the only person who touches me, for I am not allowed to mix with other prisoners or even work with them. I am like a Queen Bee, stuck in the centre of her own deadly hive and only able to watch the workers toiling in the distant fields from sunrise to sunset. Most of them are intellectuals and city workers, not peasants, and so when they return to the compound every evening they are completely exhausted. If they spot me staring at them through my barred window some of them have enough energy to summon up the hate they feel towards me and they gaze at me with eyes of loathing as if to say *you are part of that man — you are also to blame for this horror.*

When they look at me that way I have to turn away, because, deep down, I think they could be right. Yes, I am partly to blame for all of this because I am a part of him, even now. They also fear me because the way I was conceived gave me the powers of a witch. My father came home from a hunt a day earlier than expected and found my mother copulating with a python. He wanted to kill it but it spoke to him, saying that if he did my mother would die. The snake then slithered from my mother's embrace and escaped into the jungle. One month later my mother gave birth to me. Thousands of people flocked from distant villages to gaze in awe as I emerged from my soft shell. It is said that if you have sex with me my body will coil around you and seductively strangle you to death. Then I will devour you, digesting you over a week. If you wish to copulate with a woman born of a snake you must do it like a dog and the man must fill his mouth with spices because a woman born of a python is also a witch, but even that protection may not be enough and so the guard, exhilarated by fear, watches me intently to make sure I do not embrace him. He does not know that the story of my conception is a lie. One of the many my husband has spread about me.

The truth is that I was born to humans in a small village in the Highlands. My mother came from a neighbouring tribe and was bought by my father for fifty bird of paradise feathers, eight pigs and fifteen cowrie shells. She must have been beautiful when young to be worth so much. Not long after my parents were married I was born, on a night when the moon and stars were obscured by bats. This darkness

11

caused me to be born a girl and so I disappointed my parents who, naturally, wanted a boy. My father's mother was even more disappointed and because girls were not worth the total and exclusive use of a mother's milk, she forced my mother to suckle a piglet from the same tits from which I drank. The pig and I spent our first four years together, almost like brother and sister, until, at a coming-of-age ceremony, he was slaughtered in front of my eyes. My grandmother gloated over the pig's plumpness, 'This is the fattest pig I have ever seen,' she said as its stomach was slit open. I ran into the jungle, howling at its death. It was the only brother I was to have because my mother, although she could conceive, was unable to hold a baby for long. Only later did I understand the long silences and accusing looks my father gave my mother, and the whispering behind my mother's back when we were in the women's hut.

Yet, I think I was lucky being born a girl. I was allowed a greater freedom than boys my own age and I did not have to go through the terror in the men's huts from where I often heard boys crying out in fear at some ceremony they were a part of or some knowledge they were being given. Nor did I have to go through the initiation into manhood in which boys were taken to the spirit house to confront the hideous, brutal demons of adulthood; slithering, rising, ghostly, slimy, evil beings. During these ceremonies I sat with the other women in the women's hut, my hands over my ears, trying to block out the flutes of ghosts and the sounds of terror in becoming a man.

Our tribe had the most fertile garden in the whole district. This was because one of our ancestors, a giant, was jealous of his wife, a sweet, honest woman who had none of the lovers her crazed husband suspected her of having. One night he looked down at her while she slept. She looked beautiful.

12

He could not bear the thought that another man might experience such beauty so he killed her and cut up her body. He then threw the pieces onto the dead land behind the hut. Next morning the tribe was astonished to see that plants and flowers had grown from the pieces of her body and from that time on the garden became rich and fertile. I spent much of my early years there, watching my mother and the other women tend the taro, the small clutch of sugar cane, the cassava, black nightshade, amaranth and breadfruits. The women were forbidden to touch the yams and bananas as these were men's plants. Everything we wanted, we grew. While the women worked the men hunted and brought home flying foxes, cassowaries and possums to eat. I took my first steps in that garden and they were almost my last for I trod on a deadly snake and it bit me on the ankle. It was thought that I would die but, miraculously, after a week of delirium, I recovered.

Once I began to walk properly I could do pretty much as I pleased. I did not have to help my mother because all girls were spared toil until they reached puberty. Women wanted their daughters to remember a time when they didn't work, because after marriage they never stopped working. While the boys learnt to hunt, fight, obey strict taboos and call up the sacred flute spirits, I played away my childhood. I was a dreamy and adventurous child and often explored the jungle by myself. I was fascinated by the birds of paradise. I discovered where they paraded and danced and I would hide in the bushes, watching them for hours. I thought that nothing could be more beautiful than the sight of twenty males dancing excitedly on the branches, their brilliant plumes flung upward over their backs in two curving, shimmering sprays as their long tails slowly waved in counter rhythm to their quivering bodies. Others hung beneath the branches puffing out their plumes like pulsating breast shields. Their feathers were of the most extraordinary colours. Breasts of blood red, capes of yellow, plumes of velvet black and emerald green spreading around their bodies like a gorgeous skirt and crowns of feathers like the yellow or pink helmets of river gods. Their long, brilliantly coloured tails were so mysteriously beautiful that when I found a single feather that had drifted down from the clouds after a fight between two males, I hid it and returned each day to look at my treasure, feeling its weightless beauty and admiring the magical crimson and deep blue. One day I arrived and found it had gone. The bird of paradise spirit had reclaimed it. I tried to earn it back by learning to mimic the birds' calls but no matter how much I hissed, cawed or clicked nothing happened. The birds listened (I knew that because they stared at me and went quiet and moved closer along the branch towards me) but the feather never returned.

Sometimes when I got home late my mother would beat me, so worried had she been about me. She was right to be concerned. How I managed to avoid the poisonous snakes, spiders, frogs and ferocious cassowaries still astonishes me. The tribe used to laugh about my infallibility and my mother's exasperation at my wanderings. It was said by some women that a snake spirit protected me; having been unable to kill me, the snake, realising I was stronger than he, was now my protector. He not only kept me from his poisonous cousins but also from the tree ghosts and bat demons. That's where you got your story! You took something innocent and twisted it into a dark myth, so that I, too, became a concoction of your darkness.

Although I seemed to live a charmed life, the things I hated the most were bats and I made sure I was home before nightfall at which time the bats would leave their caves to head off to distant villages on killing raids. Obscuring the moon, their demonic, shrill cries pierced my very soul. Our hut was protected from these demons by a hanging basket of magic herbs, herbs I had been taught to collect by my grandmother whose husband had been killed by a bat. Sometimes lazy women did not make their herb baskets every month and their hut would be visited by the bat demon that very same night. In the morning the woman would wake to find her child or husband dead, a tell-tale trail of bat sperm on the corpse or the foul odour of bat shit coming from the dead mouth.

Once, during one of my wanderings, I caught sight of my father in the garden when my mother was in the menstruation hut. He was naked and rubbing his erect penis until its milk spurted out onto the soil. I asked my mother about this. She slapped my face good and hard for having witnessed such a sacred moment. She also made me promise never to tell anyone about what I had seen. The burden of childhood is that there is so much information to keep secret.

If I make my early years sound harsh, I do not mean to. It was a happy time. Like Christians who imagine their childhood to be like Eden, so I, too, saw my childhood as a paradise; a flowering, fertile, careless paradise. Flowering is the right word, for I was obsessed by flowers as much as I was by the birds of paradise, and I often returned from the surrounding jungle with armfuls of every sort of flower. My mother taught me to make necklaces and crowns from them and at night, while everyone was asleep, I walked the village compound covered in orchids and hibiscuses, almost drugged by their scents, while excited dogs jumped up on me and licked my face with their warm, wet tongues. At those moments I felt like the princess I saw, years later, in a procession through the streets of Sydney. She was riding on an enormous mechanical white swan. Her ecstatic eyes I knew well, for as a child I had imagined I was the most beautiful girl in the whole world; a world which I thought extended only as far as the next mist-shrouded valley. The tribe thought my behaviour strange and some said I was 'touched', as if my alliance with the snake spirit had estranged me from the rest of the world, like those who went 'peculiar' when possessed by the spirit of the swamp frog or those old people who went senile and eventually ate their own shit or vomit because they were possessed by a dog spirit.

The best spirit to have as a guardian and helpmate is the gecko. My cell gecko is a pale skin colour, with a body so translucent that I can see his beating heart. When the moon shines into my cell his eyes become like black mirrors, and they reflect me as if I were two miniature creatures locked up in his eyes for protection. It is said that if you stare into a gecko's eyes and cannot see your reflection, then you are dead. I am still alive! I checked this earlier in the evening when the guard was having sex with me. As the guard thrust himself in and out of me, the gecko came down the wall near my face, saying *tsk, tsk*, and his heart beat as fast as mine as his eyes reflected the sexual act, as if he were telling me *you are alive, you are not dreaming this moment from deep in your grave*. These bouts of lust are like fainting; entering nothingness, letting me find comfort in a brief oblivion. I thank you Mr Gecko for being here, for protecting me from my fears of death and protecting my childhood from his lies. My childhood is pulsating in my memory like your heart as if the past were a beating heart covered in the translucent skin of time.

When I was six or seven the women in the tribe started

16

to grow coffee because they had heard that down in a distant valley a white man gave white man's goods in exchange for coffee beans. Each woman had a bush to herself and occasionally a man came to our village to weigh the red beans and give goods in return. The women thought this trader was very handsome. Glossy black and tall, he looked like a warrior out of legends. He worked for the white plantation owner which made him seem even more important to us, because from what we had heard about white men they were like gods, able to fly in the sky and produce out of thin air any type of material goods you wanted. I saw a white man for the first time when I was about eleven. He was a patrol officer who arrived in our village wanting to count us. We followed him around the whole day, giggling at this phantom who wore two skins and who seemed to find supreme pleasure in counting the people, the dogs, the pigs and huts of our tribe.

'Next he'll probably want to count how many times we shit,' said one of the women and we all burst out laughing. He turned suddenly on hearing our laughter and I saw that his face was as white as bones bleached by the sun and rain. He stared at us without emotion. We stepped back, nervous, because such emotionless masks are worn by sorcerers who use them to keep their deadly thoughts to themselves. The white man stayed overnight and left the following morning but during the night some of the braver boys had stolen objects belonging to him. I was desperate to see them but they were put in the spirit house which was taboo for women. I heard about one object that was so sharp that it could cut a cloud in two or separate two layers of skin. My curiosity about this tiny instrument was so great that I did something unforgivable.

A few nights after the patrol officer left I curled up in

the corner of the hut pretending to sleep while my mother drank my father's strength and then, once they were asleep, I crept outside. I wore a skirt of pandanus leaves to stop the bat spirit from entering my vagina. I was afraid that the dogs sleeping around the glowing embers of the fires would wake and bark at me but I passed unnoticed. The giant spirit house was an A-shaped building that had an entrance resembling a gaping mouth. Inside was everything I was forbidden to see. Because I wasn't a woman yet and did not have the deadly stink of menstruation, I reasoned that I would not harm the white man's objects. As I approached the entrance I began to sweat with fear. Not only was it taboo for a girl to see inside the spirit house but inside were deadly spirits and it required a will of great power not to be overwhelmed by them. The boys' cries when they underwent initiation testified to that. My body shook as I approached the mouth but I did not stop, my soul was consumed with a lust for the forbidden.

The excited moonlight vanished when I entered the spirit house and I was swallowed up by darkness. I wanted to cry out but my fear of being discovered was greater. My nostrils were filled with the strong odours of men. Gradually my eyes made out figures. They were huge ghosts; enormous bug-eyed creatures who encircled me, preparing to eat me. I was paralysed with fright. My heart beat so hard and fast that I thought it would explode from my stomach. I wanted to flee but my legs felt as if they had rooted themselves into the dirt floor. The creatures began to whirl around me, their huge mouths opening and closing silently and then, suddenly, lightly, one touched me. I fainted onto the floor.

'What are you doing in here?' a voice asked. I awoke to find myself at the feet of the alligator spirit; his long, ferocious mouth was about to tear me apart. I knew I must answer him truthfully as it was the only way to save myself.

'Did you come here to spy on male business and secrets?'

'I'm sorry, Alligator Spirit, but I didn't come to spy on you. I came to see the white man's things.'

'And that's the truth?'

I was so scared that I could not answer. I pissed myself and my body shook. The Alligator Spirit's teeth glinted in the moonlight that oozed in between the wooden slabs of the wall. I cringed, knowing I was about to be eaten. From out of its bowels stepped a smaller figure. 'Palu, what are you doing here?'

For a moment I thought I was dreaming. The voice sounded like my father and the shadowy figure looked like him. It came closer. It was my father. He picked me up. I could see he was very angry with me, but I didn't care. 'Protect me from the spirits,' I cried and pushed my face into his chest.

'They've gone,' he said quietly. I lifted my head and looked around me. There was no need to be afraid anymore, the spirits, both good and bad, had vanished and were replaced by their fake wooden selves.

My poor father! Fancy having a daughter like me. I had broken one of the strictest taboos and yet he wouldn't denounce me because I was of his blood and I realised, for the first time, that he liked me, even loved me in his own male way. The problem was that he wanted a boy to teach and admire and be proud of but all he could do was love me because there was nothing to teach me. 'As you're already here, Palu, I'll show you the white man's objects, then we'll go.' He took me to the centre of the spirit house where a table had been set up. A hole in the roof had been made so that the moon and starlight fell directly on it and the two metallic objects shone darkly. Touching them with reverence, my father murmured 'so sharp... so sharp'. He explained their use to me: 'They rub them over their face to cut off their beards but it doesn't cut their flesh. Their faces become as smooth as a baby's bum.' I was as awestruck as my father. He showed me other things. A metal container which had its lid partly removed so that it curled up like a frozen tongue. Attached to the tongue was a thin metal object like a stiff worm. I touched the tongue, it felt cold and alien. 'He doesn't need to catch fish from the river, he makes them grow in this box.' We gazed at the magical metal box, amazed by the white man's sorcery. 'And this,' he said, holding up to the light something that looked like the pale skin of a baby snake, 'is something mysterious.' My father placed two fingers into it and shook his head.

'Maybe it's to put coffee beans in?' I said.

'Too small,' he said, carefully putting it back in its place. 'It's probably something magical made out of the skin of a white man he killed.'

I felt as if I were standing before an altar of extraordinary magic, magic much more potent and mysterious than that of our sorcerer.

'And what are those,' I asked my father, pointing to a collection of white, peculiarly shaped stones, the size of men's fists, which was at the head of the table, shrouded in shadows, guarding the white man's things. My father, woken from his contemplation of the strange skin-like object, looked at the stones and then back at me. I could see that he was debating with himself whether he should tell me about them. In some ways they were even more mysterious and fascinating than the white man's objects. Even a ten-year-old girl knows how to get a man to do things for her, and I smiled sweetly. 'Please, I want to know.' My father yearned to pass on knowledge to a son but I was the only child he had. Caught up in the spell of the white man's articles he found himself breaking another taboo, one even more serious than allowing me to stay inside the spirit house.

'If I tell you, will you tell me how you talk to the birds of paradise? I know you do because I saw you talking to them the other day. I thought I was stalking a bird of paradise by its call but it was you talking to them.'

My father knew that if he could talk to the birds of paradise he would be able to capture them and become rich by the sale of their feathers. My desire to know about the stones and his desire to be rich had the same urgency and we agreed to help each other. He explained to me that the stones were the tribe's dreamstones and were the shapes of various animals and mountains. Before going to sleep a man would touch the stone he wanted to dream about. If he dreamt of Galos mountain it meant he would scale its peak and find the cassowary. Once he had scaled the mountain and captured the bird in his sleep then it would happen in reality. 'These stones have been with our tribe since the beginning of time and only men know about them.' He fondled the bird stone. 'I will dream about talking to the bird of paradise tonight and the dreamstone will make it happen.' He put the bird dreamstone back with the others and we left the spirit house. Walking back to our hut we said nothing but we both knew we should never, ever talk to anyone, not even to each other, about this night of sacrilege.

I kept my promise to my father. Secretly I taught him how birds of paradise talk. In mimicking them he drew them within spear range and soon began to kill many, collecting their brilliant feathers and selling them to the coffee bean man in exchange for new axes, knives and other things. People became jealous of my father's sudden prowess and they said he had made a deal with a bat demon. My father told no one how he was so successful and so many rumours spread about him. Some village women thought it odd that he often took me into the jungle to teach me how to use a bow and arrow or spear. They felt sorry for him, thinking that such actions were a sign of his desperation for a son and blamed my mother. Normally men and women led separate lives and my father and I were destroying this arrangement. The things he taught me were not taboo (for instance, he didn't teach me to play the sacred flutes) and so he was not criticised for this, only pitied that he should want to pass on male skills to his daughter. I should have realised that there was something wrong in our relationship. Also I should have realised that our sacrilegious night together had made us more vulnerable to demon spirits. However, at the time I didn't care; I felt privileged in becoming my father's companion.

I accompanied my father to his killing spots and helped him pluck the dead birds. I felt proud, like he did, of our new wealth. Our hut now had brand new axes, picks, knives, cans of honey, a white lady's hat for my mother and a white man's shirt which my father wore on important ceremonial occasions. Such conspicious wealth annoyed a few people but my father and I didn't care, we were locked in our secret world and we looked down on our envious critics.

In our excursions to collect the feathers my father took to calling me Palo, the male equivalent of my name. I took little notice of this, thinking it was a joke, but other curious things began to happen. He grew annoyed with me if I squatted when I pissed. He also hated my growing breasts and one time, as we gutted some birds, he turned on me, suddenly and inexplicably, and slapped me hard, so hard that I almost fainted from the pain. 'You're such a girl,' he spat, sending red betel nut juice over my breasts. 'Why are you such a girl!'

People began to notice his changing behaviour. From being a mild-mannered man, he became argumentative, even aggressive, yelling at people and challenging young men to duels over petty or imagined slights. I grew apprehensive, seeing him lose his self-control so frequently. At night he did not wait for me to go to sleep before forcing my mother to drain his penis. He became abusive and rough during sex and took to calling my mother's vagina 'a dead moon'. One night when my mother was sucking his penis, my father looked over at me and smiled mysteriously, as if to say, 'We are bonded together you and I and whatever we do, we do together. We both hate the dead moon sucking my manhood.'

The smile scared me because it seemed so crazy. I sensed he was possessed by a bat. His eyes were shiny and demonic like a bat's. Then it struck me; my father was paying the cost for having allowed me to break tribal taboos. His smile paralysed me and made me vulnerable. The bat demon spirit knew it too and he penetrated me, crawling quickly, viciously, up through my vagina. He took over my brain and I saw myself, like a snake that has crawled out of its old skin and is looking back at the vestiges of its other self. This other self saw my crazed father and my mother choking on his penis, while my former self was detached and calm, being stroked and soothed by the sweet-talking bat spirit inside her. A normal girl would have cried out in alarm at what was happening to her or turned away from her father's gaze but I was bewitched.

After expending himself in my mother's mouth, my father pushed her away and clutching his still erect wet penis said, 'Palu, you will grow one of these. You will become a boy

23

and we will tell everyone that a miracle has happened. By breaking the taboo we have done right.'

His voice was soft and certain and he seemed even more demented for being unemotional. My mother did not know what was happening and I could barely breathe as the bat demon was everywhere in the hut, its musty smell suffocating me. I became one again when the bat demon returned to my father, who grabbed my hand and placed it on his penis and with his other hand clutched my vagina. 'It will grow,' he murmured sweetly, 'and you, my son, will come with me to the spirit house.'

Although afraid I also felt pity for my father because I knew that the burden of having broken the taboos had in turn broken him. My mother screamed at my father to let me go. 'Stop doing such filthy things!'

My father nodded as if in agreement and winked at me as if to say *we know the truth, don't we? And we know what to do!* He let go of me, picked up a new axe, and in one powerful swing brought it down on my mother's head, splitting it open. Blood and brains splattered us, like a melon exploding after being thrown against a rock. Her body squirmed as good and bad spirits fought over it. Calmly my father spread his arms like a bat, smiling at me all the while, and then headed outside with his axe. A few people had awoken when they heard my mother's screams and were running towards our hut to see what had happened. I crept past the quivering body to the doorway. My father was observing the people heading towards him. I knew he was inwardly laughing at them, like a bat hanging from a tree, looking down on the tiny people below and feeling invincible and superior.

'My shirt,' he commanded, like a warrior asking for a battle shield. I crept back past my dead mother, grabbed the white

24

man's shirt and took it outside. Not caring that it was stained with his wife's blood and brains, my father put on the shirt and marched towards the hut of an old man who had slighted him in the morning by calling him a 'woman lover'. I knew he was going to kill the old man because I could feel my father's hate. I called out to him to stop. By this stage people had seen the slaughter in our hut and women were keening loudly. Things, however, were happening so fast that no one knew what to do; only my father had purpose.

I screamed at him: 'It's my fault, I forced you to break the taboo!'

But bats do not listen to a virgin's voice. He disappeared into the hut with his bloody axe. There was a woman's scream and the thudding of the axe. My father reappeared, followed by the old man's wife, covered in blood, screaming out, 'He killed my husband!' Her voice pierced my father's thoughts and, irritated, he turned around and axed her neck. She fell, her head still partly attached to her body and her eyes popping in surprise. The noise of the barking excited dogs, howling children, screaming women and yelling men had become overwhelming.

My father gazed disinterestedly at the frightened crowd and walked towards a young man who, a few days before, had told my father that he must have made a pact with the demon spirit to have become rich so quickly. My father raised his bloody axe but got no further. A spear pierced his side. He dropped his axe and stared quizzically at the wound. Smiling at his assailant he pulled the spear from his side and bent down to pick up his axe. Galvanised into action by the throwing of the spear the men started shooting arrows at my father. Dozens landed in his body. He screamed out in pain. His screams were high-pitched, demonic, unhuman. I echoed his shrill pain, crying out, 'No, it was my fault!' But my words could not stop the arrows. He fell onto the ground in a kneeling position, looking like a spiny ant-eater that has half transformed itself into a human being. I ran to him. His dead eyes were open and clear — the bat demon had gone. My father had found release.

I have to calm down. Have to calm down! I tell myself to calm down but remembering that night is difficult. My gecko is in the moonlight, his heart beating gently. I try and match my heartbeat with his. Outside I hear the guards laughing and gossiping and in the background is a radio which they are only half listening to. The familiar voice drifts to me down the corridor:

'I will break your arms and feed the birds with your shit. Bats will drink your blood. Look out, I am everywhere. I am the phantom, the ghost who walks. I am here to protect you from evil...'

I don't strain to hear anymore. A guard is snoring softly nearby. He wakes occasionally to slap a mosquito. Where is the guard who fucks me? Is he outside with the men bragging about what he does to the President's wife? Probably. Men like to brag about their conquests, whether they be other countries or women.

In order to see if the death of my parents had rid my soul of the evil my taboo-breaking had caused, a sorcerer was brought in from a neighbouring tribe. He knelt beside me and took some herbs out of his string bag which he put into his mouth and chewed thoroughly. Then he put his marshy smelling mouth against mine and passed, a little bit at a time, the brown pulp into my mouth. When I had finished swallowing the last of it he stepped away and looked at me closely as if looking into my very soul. As he stared at me his pupils began slowly to disappear up behind his forehead until only the whites of his eyes remained. His body began to shake until it jerked so violently it seemed as if he would explode. His mouth yawned as wide open as an alligator's and from out of it he pulled a long strip of cloth. He showed it to the tribe who were gathered in a semi-circle around me. He told them he had extracted it from my stomach and that it was a sign of how my family and I had too many white men's goods. This love of such objects was caused by an evil spirit which still resided in me. To get rid of it he took me down to the river where he washed me so hard he rubbed my skin raw. As I stood in the deep water I looked back at the tribe on the bank. They stared at me passively, no sympathy in their eyes. After an hour or so the sorcerer stopped rubbing me and walked out of the river, telling the tribe that I would always be a bad influence and there was nothing he could do to help me. He suspected that I was really a changeling and that when I was a baby a demon had crept into the garden while my mother was working and had taken the real Palu and substituted a demon. 'That girl,' he said, pointing at me as I stood in the swollen river, 'is a changeling and you must get rid of her or else she'll destroy the tribe.'

The next day the coffee bean man arrived and threw me onto the back of his truck on top of the hard bags of coffee. Those members of the tribe who had escorted me to the dirt road watched me without emotion. They were glad to be rid of me. I had broken important taboos and had caused disaster. I knew that behind those white faces of mourning a few were thinking it would have been better to kill me than send me off to become a servant on the coffee plantation. I would not have cared if they had killed me. I had felt nothing since the slaughter. The truck set off down the rough

27

track and I bounced around like a sack of taro. If I had not been so exhausted and so empty I would have been curious, even scared of what lay before me.

Near twilight we arrived down in the valley. It was unlike any valley I had ever seen or imagined. Instead of jungle and forest, it was an enormous plain of coffee bean bushes stretching to the setting sun. In the distant corner of the plantation was a white man's house, looking like a giant white toad. I grew afraid as the truck headed down the long driveway towards its glowing eyes. We were met by a brown woman who lifted me down from the truck, slapped my body free of dust and spoke to me harshly in an unknown language. The truck drove off and the woman motioned me into the house. I shook my head; I was terrified by its strangeness and its monstrous size. The woman grabbed me by the hand and dragged me up the wooden steps which creaked and moaned at every touch and when she opened the front door it squeaked like an animal in pain. Inside the light was so intense that I had to squint. It was like entering the cave of a million of fireflies. We walked down a long tunnel towards awful music and then entered a room where we stopped.

'Mista Bee,' said the woman to the man in the corner with his back to us. The man stopped fondling the teeth of a large brown box and the music ceased. He turned and faced me, his eyes an unnatural blue. His clothes were white, his face white and even his hair was pure white. Oh, my god, my god! I recognise this man. This is the bat demon. This is the lair of the king of the bat demons! You will know the bat demon, my father once told me, because he will be white all over and his eyes as blue as the sky. He is white because he has been living in a cave of evil, sending his minions out to corrupt the human soul. My skirt of pandanus leaves rustled loudly as my body shook in fear. The king of the bat demons said something to me. I pissed myself and fainted onto the hard floor.

I woke to a world beyond dreams, a world of magic and mystery, a world where water came when you turned a metal handle, where beds were above the floor, where floors were covered in coloured fur, where water was cooled in a box, where music came from flat black discs, where food was eaten from a table and where voices spoke into a black stick from the end of the world.

Although I missed my parents terribly I quickly fitted into this new world and began to feel as if my luck had changed. I enjoyed this wonderland and felt like the changeling the sorcerer had accused me of being, except this time I had been taken by a good spirit and placed in a glorious garden. I was taught to bathe by the woman who first met me, the housekeeper Maz. She also taught me how to wear a dress. I liked my simple cotton frock (with its strange animals of long necks and brown spots printed all over it) so much so that I even wore it to bed, unaware of how ugly the wrinkles made it look the next day. Maz taught me how to sew, to cook, do the laundry and polish the silver. Through her I picked up pidgin English, a language Mister Bee loathed and spoke only reluctantly, according to Maz. Some of the plantation workers taught me foul words and I used them unknowingly in front of Maz who, having been brought up by Christian missionaries, despaired of me.

Maz was one of eight household servants. She was Mister Bee's favourite and it was she who served his food, made his bed and made him comfortable. Although Mister Bee was kind to me on the few times we were accidentally in each other's presence, I was still afraid of him. To have all those people working for him made him all the more powerful. You know it, don't you, how the more people who serve you, the more powerful you seem to be, and the more powerful you seem to be, the more powerful you are.

Sometimes when I was not working I saw Mister Bee strolling through his plantation, his white, floppy hat weaving through the top of the coffee bushes, a dozen or so workers following him, wanting to serve his every wish. Even in the house everyone spoke of him as if he were a god. They talked, too, of his strictness. If things were done wrongly he would not yell at the culprit but look at him coldly. If the same mistake were made again then he would get rid of the wrongdoer. Once he had been less aloof and more warm but that was years ago when his wife and daughter had been with him. They had returned to Australia, leaving him alone in this country they despised for its lack of comforts and white people.

At night Mister Bee played the piano and after he had eaten dinner (always alone unless a patrol officer or buyer turned up) he listened to records, terrible music that sounded like angry insects by a river. I knew all this from Maz who gave the information reluctantly as if she were passing on taboo knowledge. I nagged her about him because I knew that the more I learnt about him the more human he would become, just as the more people know about you, the less godlike you will become. I liked to help Bokelolu do the washing because I could inspect Mister Bee's clothes. It comforted me to know that he shat and pissed like other humans. I also liked helping Maz make up his bedroom because I could see what was in his drawers, in his wardrobe and on the mantelpiece. I used to stare at the photographs of his wife and daughter and imagine what sort of women they were. Tall and serious, they looked like wooden statues to which the carver had failed to give expressions. Mister Bee

30

wasn't in these pictures. Maz told me he was the long shadow at their feet taking the photograph. This information made Mister Bee even more clever than I thought. He had captured their souls with the magic camera but his still ran free.

I loved those first months on the plantation. Of course I did not work as hard as the others, especially the pickers, because I was still young. I was also lucky in that Maz, who was unmarried because she had devoted most of her life to Mister Bee, looked upon me as a foster child and so I got away with much rudeness and laziness. I swanned around poking my nose into whatever business took my fancy, yapping incessantly.

One night when Maz was sick with some sort of fever, she got me to serve Mister Bee his dinner. 'If you make a mistake it will be because you're a child — he would not forgive an adult.' The other servants were almost as worried as I was when they heard who was to serve the master. Their nervousness made me feel a tremendous responsibility, so much so that I nearly fainted as I walked down the corridor to the dining room. He was playing that horrid piano as I entered the room. My hands were wet with sweat and the tray felt as if it could slip at any moment. I walked to the table, the objects on the tray rattling like bones. Mister Bee had his back to me as he played. I was like a gecko, ready to run if he showed the slightest movement towards me. I laid out the cutlery as I had been taught and put the bowl of breadfruit soup in the correct place but just as I was about to sneak out, the music stopped. I turned and saw him staring directly at me. A gaze so powerful and a spirit so overbearing that my hands went limp and the tray fell to the floor. There was a clatter as it hit, then silence. I did not know what to do.

'Pick it up,' he commanded. I obeyed him immediately,

like one of those soulless people who are at the command of sorcerers. He stood up and walked towards me. For the first time I saw just how old he was. I had never been so close to him before (or maybe my eyes had always focused on the ground in his presence) and I saw that his white cheeks were marked with tiny purple veins like unravelling balls of string. His eyes were weary, as if he had not slept for weeks and his back slightly bent as if carrying a burden. He sat with a sigh. I prepared to leave the room but he told me to stay. I stood trembling before him, believing he was going to tell me what a bad job I had done and how Maz had let him down by using me for such duties.

'No more pidgin. Pidgin is arse tok. Got it?'

Even though I didn't quite understand what he meant I nodded as if I had. Did he want me not to speak to him or not to use pidgin? Either way, how could I reply?

'You speak English! Got it?' He then waved me from the room.

I ran down the corridor like a whirlwind, forgetting such behaviour was forbidden, and rushed outside to the shack where I slept with Maz. She had wanted me to report to her after each course but she was too ill to tell me what to do and could only repeat deliriously, 'Mista Bee, manbird'.

I returned to the house, not knowing what to say to him if he asked me anything again. I resolved to say nothing and when I served the main course I held my tongue so tightly between my teeth that I thought I would bite right through it. I backed away after serving him but he motioned me to stay, looking at me with those terrifying blue eyes and pointing to one of the chairs. Thinking he wanted to sit on a different chair I pulled it out for him and waited for him to move. He grew annoyed and pointed at the chair, saying loudly, 'Sit!' I did as I was told and sat, frozen still, gazing at the white lace table cloth so I wouldn't have to look at his creepy eyes.

'You have kai-kai with me. Got it?' I thought I had misheard him so I said nothing.

'Yes or no? Night-time. Kai-kai.'

Not knowing what to say I stared at the tablecloth, wanting it to swallow me up as it was now doing to an insect that had fallen into an abyss between the lace.

'Palu? You understand me? Kai-kai bilong me or whatever the bloody phrase is.'

My mouth was dry with fear. What did he want with me? I nodded and it seemed to satisfy him.

'Good. You start to speak English tomorrow. Now ske-daddle out of here, I want to eat in peace tonight.'

From then on, every night, I came to his table, a frightened thirteen-year-old black girl, not long out of the jungle, and there I was taught to use a knife and fork and to speak English. The whole plantation was astonished at this development. Not for the last time were there rumours that I was a witch. Some workers said I had enchanted Mister Bacon by putting some special potion in his food that night. It had to be the only explanation because how else could a girl, just out of the jungle, sit at the boss's table as if she were his daughter. Maz was the most bewildered of all. 'Did you bewitch him?' she asked and when I said I hadn't an awful thought struck her. 'You didn't offer him your body did you?' The idea was so absurd that I laughed at her. I couldn't help her figure out why Mister Bee had done this because I didn't know myself.

Having no explanations all I could do was enthrall the household staff with descriptions of my dinners with Mister Bacon (now that I was learning English I had to use his proper surname). After the dinners I would sit on the top bunk of a room in the shack I shared with Maz and, with my legs swinging back and forth in delight at being the centre of attention, I would tell them how he had taught me to eat with a knife and fork and how, if food dribbled down the side of your mouth, you used a piece of cloth to wipe it away. Bokelolu nodded wisely when she heard this piece of information. 'That would explain the food stains on those pieces of cloth when I do the laundry,' she said, and everyone giggled excitedly at another mystery solved about our master. As time went on I became big-headed and looked down on the others. Soon they grew scared to criticise me for fear I would dob them in and tried to butter me up by giving me small gifts. This made me even more impossible to be with.

This is not to say that Mister Bacon and I were close. I was still partly afraid of him and our relationship was more like teacher and pupil than anything else. We started my English by identifying the cutlery and naming objects around us. I impressed him with my quickness and concentration. After the main course was finished Mister Bacon would get out a pen and paper and a book, usually the Bible, and teach me to read and write. He must have been an exceptionally lonely man to do this. After an hour of English he would say goodnight and I would leave him to play his awful music and drink whiskey. As my reading improved he gave me a novel with drawings in it called *Gulliver's Travels*, knowing full well that this story of giants and midgets would appeal to me. Slowly, bit by aching bit, I read it, believing that Swift's story was true. After finishing it I went to the stables where Mister Bacon kept two horses and spent a morning trying to talk to them. They listened but stubbornly refused to reply. I reasoned that they might not have under-stood me because they were European creatures. After Swift I was given Dickens, a favourite of Mister Bacon's and which I also came to adore. I stayed in my bunk until late morning reading these novels while everyone worked. Oh, God, I could be a lazy little thing!

Although I learnt English extremely quickly I seemed to have no head for numbers. Mister Bacon was patient with me and tried to teach me addition and subtraction using the cutlery. I grew so tired of separating and putting together piles of cutlery that I wanted to cry out for mercy and hated the white man for having invented these instruments of mental torture that made me look so stupid. 'Oh, why don't they just eat with their fingers!' I thought to myself after each evening of fruitless lessons to teach me to count.

Then, one night, Mister Bacon put a spoon next to three others on the table. 'That makes four,' he said with a sigh, tiring of trying to teach me to count. And it suddenly came to me! Three and one makes four! One and three makes four! It was like magic. I had learnt the magic of numbers! I gathered together all the cutlery on the table and feverishly started counting. I realised you could count anything! Too excited to sit still, I ran from the table and, like a piece of paper caught in the wind, I blew through the house, counting the rooms, the dogs outside, the chairs, the trees, my fingers and toes. I was crazed by numbers.

When they saw me counting the trees the workers thought I was possessed by a genial spirit who was mischievously playing with me. 'Look,' I said to them as they sat near the processing plant under the moon, 'I have five toes on my foot!' They laughed but I didn't care. I rushed back inside to my teacher. Look, Mister Bacon, I have two ears and two eyes and my two eyes are seeing you laughing for the first time. You are laughing at me and with me and I am bouncing the moon with happiness.

One night I was awoken from my sleep by Maz. 'Come, Mista Bee wants you. Quickie. Quickie!' Agitated, she pulled me from my bunk, sending the copy of *David Copperfield* I had been reading before falling asleep flying onto the concrete floor. I cried out and jumped down to rescue the precious object but Maz pulled me away from it and threw a dress over me. As she hurried me down the corridor towards the living room I grew worried. Was this frenzy of Maz because of something she had done or I had done? What was wrong? I was worried he might expel me and expulsion was my greatest fear. I was far too happy there to want to go anywhere else.

A record was playing loudly when we entered the living room. Mister Bacon was standing, shakily, in the middle of the room, one hand holding on to the back of a chair as if the earth were moving and he was trying to steady himself. In the other hand he had a glass. 'Here Mista Bee, got Palu.' He nodded and waved Maz out of the room. Only later did I learn that this night was one of Mister Bacon's drunken binges. When isolation and loneliness became too heavy a burden for him he drank a bottle of scotch and did strange things. One time he had to be stopped from pouring kerosene onto the coffee bushes and setting fire to them.

'You'll end up with huge feet like Maz,' he said, pointing at my bare feet with his glass of scotch. 'Come with me.'

I followed him down the corridor to a locked door. This was the room I knew to be his daughter's. It was always kept clean by Maz but no one else was allowed in. After cleaning it she locked the door and returned the key to her master.

Mister Bacon turned on the light. I blinked at the brightness. Unlike the other drab colours of the house this room was painted in bright pinks and soft whites. He thumped the wardrobe. 'There, try on a dress that fits you. Get some shoes, too, then come and see me when you're dressed.' He left me and returned to the living room. I looked around at this beautiful room, unable to believe anything could be so richly decorated. Pictures of princesses, flowers and English royalty were stuck on the wall. The bed was covered in bright pink blankets and three lovely dolls sat up against the fluffy pillows like bewitched children. I could have stood staring open-mouthed for hours but I remembered I had better hurry. I quickly tried on a dress and it fitted me well. The real problem was the shoes. They were all too narrow for my feet. I managed to force the largest pair on but even those made my feet feel as if they were in the grip of a crocodile's jaw. They were so tight and painful I could barely walk. I gazed at myself in the mirror. My white, frilly dress was beautiful. I felt like one of those dolls on the bed. I hobbled out into the living room and stood before Mister Bacon who was sitting in his leather armchair.

'Shoes too tight?'

'A teensy bit, Mister Bacon.'

'Doesn't matter, you'll learn to wear them. The dress looks good. Matter of fact, you look as beautiful as a piccaninny princess.'

Pleased by his comments, I smiled. He pointed to the chair opposite and told me to sit in it. As he drank he talked, speaking of many things I did not understand properly; of his wife and daughter (how he loved them, how they hated him), how I reminded him of a pretty piccaninny he had once seen on his parents' Queensland farm as a boy. He spoke of prospecting for gold in my country and of how he was the first white man to penetrate this area. I tried to concentrate on what he was saying but sometimes the pain of the shoes was so great that I barely stopped from crying out. Only near dawn when he had finished his scotch did he stop talking. Before falling asleep in his chair he smiled at me and said, 'Irene'. Confused by drink and what I was wearing, he had mistaken me for his daughter.

His drunkenness had unleashed some private desire which he had wanted to express, and now that he had allowed it freedom it could never be constrained again. I was given the key to his daughter's room and allowed to wear anything I liked. I remember the peculiarly dead smell of her clothes which had lain in lavender and moth balls for over a decade, awaiting her return. Until the smell faded with use I felt as if I were wearing the clothes of a corpse. I had to wear a different dress every day and present myself to Mister Bacon before breakfast. I was also forced to wear the hard leather shoes until my toes curled in on themselves but gradually I got used to them. Nowadays it is a standard joke that you can tell those who have had a Western upbringing by their deformed toes. And that is another black mark against me, isn't it, my dear husband. Remember how you fondled my toes and cursed what the shoes had done to them but also how you loved me wearing Western high heels. I hear myself; click, clacking across the tiles of the palace, looking for you, wanting to talk, just talk, but you are the phantom. Click, clack, let me find the ghost who walks. Let me press my forehead against you. If you won't talk then at least pass on your thoughts to me. Let me press my head against your head so I can feel the blood pulsating through your skin so I know you are alive and not just a walking corpse. Click, clack on Western high heels, like some sad drummer beating on a hollow log. Talk to me. Mister Bacon talked to me.

38

He told me of his upbringing on an Australian farm and I told him of my life before he took me in. Sometimes we would talk for hours on the veranda which overlooked his magnificent plantation and, if he had drunk more than his usual three scotches, he would grow nostalgic and tell me of his days prospecting for gold. What a strange pair we must have looked. Mister Bacon's eyes were so poor he could not see, as I could, those inquisitive workers who hid in the nearby coffee bushes watching us, listening to our incomprehensible language that floated over to them in the languid, warm air. How they must have envied me and puzzled over my managing to assume the position of Mister Bacon's daughter as if, in my blackness, I had become the carbon imprint of his off-spring.

He got me to read to him and there, in that lonely house, thousands of miles from Western civilisation, I read his favourite Victorian novels aloud. The awkwardness of my position sometimes bewildered me and after leaving him I would toss and turn in my bunk, excited and confused. It was difficult living in two worlds and it was made worse by the fact that every night I had to leave behind the dress I had worn that day and return to my dirty shack wearing my drab cotton frock. This began to rankle me so much that I eventually took a young worker as a lover. This boy took my virginity and said sweet, stupid things in my ear but he was just a convenience, like the guard. He thought he was taking advantage of me when, in reality, it was me who was using him to make me forget my confusion. I try to recall this young man's face but I cannot. I always associate him with the night because it was then, after I had talked and read to Mister Bacon, that we met and fucked amid the rows of coffee bushes. In me he found a girl he could possess without any responsibility and, of course, the sexual tang was sweeter because he was taking a girl whom he felt to be uppity. Like all men, he thought that by taking me sexually he would bring me down to his level. He was just like my guard. Perhaps the boy died and was reincarnated as the guard?

One morning as I stood before the wardrobe mirror modelling a dress I was still undecided about, Mister Bacon burst into the room, his face as pink as a young coffee cherry, and grabbing my arm, squeezed it so tightly I thought he would snap it in two. He yelled at me 'Have you been with a boy?' A sense of wrongdoing flooded me and I looked away.

'You have been with a worker. Who was it?'

'Wauru.'

He twisted my arm so that I was forced to look at him. 'You are a little whore, Palu. A slut,' he shouted, spraying my face with angry spittle.

'I'm sorry, Mista Bee.'

'Mister Bacon!'

'Mister Bacon.'

Unable to look him in the eyes I stared straight ahead at his chest and the thin white hairs which poked up out of the top of his shirt, hoping he would stop abusing me. 'Do you want to end up a whore? After all I've taught you — you go around like a bitch on heat.' He went on and on. Finally I could take the pain and disgrace no more.

'Mister Bacon, I'm hurting.'

My words stopped him. He was suddenly aware of how tightly he was squeezing my arm. He let go and stepped away. I was not ashamed of having had sex with Wauru but I did feel shame at having hurt this man who had allowed me to live in paradise. 'I'm sorry, Mister Bacon, it will not happen again.' He looked at me as if not believing me. A thought struck me. Who told him of my affair? Maz was the only person who knew. I understood, then, how jealous she must have been of me. For years she had been the only person close to her Mista Bee and now a young girl had taken her place and pushed her into the background. Even though I understood why she was jealous I hated Maz at that moment and wanted to kill her.

Mister Bacon slumped on the pink bed, exhausted. 'How you have disappointed me, Palu. You people have no self-control.' I got down on my knees and begged his forgiveness as I had learnt to do from those Dickens novels I had read aloud to him. 'Don't, Palu, get up!' But I couldn't and wouldn't because I was terrified he was going to throw me off the plantation. The thought frightened me so much that I prostrated myself before him like an errant tribesman before his chief and I began to speak the required formula of abjection in my own tongue. I called him my father, my protector, my chief and my master. I told him I was a piece of dog shit and I wasn't worthy to lick his bum. Mister Bacon, not understanding the words, but realising the extent of my submission to him, tried to make me stop but I was hysterical. Embarrassed by my behaviour he stood up and moved away from the bed, looking at me in the mirror as if my reflection somehow made me easier to deal with. When I stopped my bubbling and was quiet he said softly, 'Would you like to live in this house?' Mr Gecko, do you want to know a young girl's happiness? There I am, in my yellow chiffon dress, jumping up from the floor as if catapulted and I'm running to him wanting to hug him but I think he wouldn't want me touching him so, in an agony of joy that wants to explode, I tear out of the room, screeching, 'Yes, yes!' The other girls stop in their tracks as I run up and down the corridor and out onto the veranda and they say to each other, 'What in the heck has got into Palu now?'

The daughter's room became mine. I knew the price; I was not allowed to see Wauru again or mix too much with my own kind. As far as I was concerned this was a bargain. I was living in heaven. Look at me on that first night, sleeping in my soft pink cloud hugging my three fairy babies. Look at that smile, it's on my face even when I sleep. Counting my lucky stars would have been impossible, there were as many as in a clear night sky.

Not long after I had shifted into the house Wauru knocked on my window. He was wearing the crimson hibiscus of a courting lover in his hair. I answered his pleas and randy dancing by threatening to have Mister Bacon get rid of him. He slunk away into the night and whenever I saw him afterwards he looked at me with real hate in his eyes. I didn't care, I smiled back at him with the condescending smile of a royal towards her servant.

Mister Bacon wanted someone to type his letters so he taught me to use a typewriter. He had become a different man, finding a real happiness in teaching me. He took me on tours of the plantation and gave me books on growing coffee. Who wants to know about coffee? Well, there is Palu; she's a real clever dick and she'll tell you whether you want to know or not. Mister Bacon's coffee is *Coffea arabica*, whereas the coffee grown in the lowlands is the inferior *Coffea canephora*. Pests? Well, there are the stem-girdler weevils, leafrollers and leafhoppers. Diseases? There is coffee rust (*Hemileia vastatrix*) but it occurs in other countries, so not to worry. There are also the various methods of transforming the bright red cherry into a miniature model of a dark brown vagina. Ho hum, there is fifteen-year-old

Palu boring the pants off the servants with all these facts as they try to prepare dinner in the kitchen. I must have been a real pain in the bum. Coffee had become my world because I had to impress Mister Bacon if I were going to become, as I wanted to, his right-hand man.

Rumours of my growing importance quickly filtered through the district and one day some members of my tribe arrived on the front veranda. They asked me if I would give them white man's goods such as radios and saws. I was annoyed by their visit, fearing that Mister Bacon, who was overseeing spraying down in the backblocks, might see these people and, thinking I belonged to them, send me back to them. I was also angry with them for coming and asking me for gifts when they had exiled me. I quickly sent them packing. Their arse grass, primitive ways and dirty bodies offended me. They left, more confused than annoyed. After they had gone I felt no remorse, only a sense of relief that Mister Bacon had not seen them.

Occasionally a patrol officer or buyer would pass through. Mister Bacon never explained my presence, taking it for granted, and after dinner he would show me off by having me recite his favourite poem, 'Ripperty! Kye! A-hoo!', by Henry Lawson.

> There was a young woman, as I've heard tell
> (Ripperty! Kye! A-hoo!)
> Lived near the sea in a nice little hell
> That she made for herself and her husband as well;
> But that's how a good many married folk dwell —
> Ripperty! Kye! A-hoo!

I hated that first verse because it made marriage seem so awful but I loved the way the poem finished:

Now there's a young woman, as I've heard tell
(*Sing gently*): Ripperty! Kye! A-hoo!
Lives near the sea in a nice little shell,
(*Sing softly*): Ripperty! Kye! A-hoo!
That's built of brick, wood, and red tiles, at Rozelle;
She's fond of her husband and he's doing well —
And — that's how a good many married folk dwell.
(*Sing exultantly*) Ripperty! Kye! A-hoo!

I would take Lawson's instructions to heart and yell out, exultantly, 'Ripperty! Kye! A-hoo!'

A guard has just visited me wondering if I am mad. 'Why are you singing and smiling,' he asked.

'Because I'm remembering the good times.'

He shrugged. Such a reply is a definite sign of madness. As his footsteps faded down the corridor I heard a voice on a distant radio. That screechy white girl's voice. The galah is singing:

> We should work harder
> To help our country
> We should work harder
> To help you and me.

I see you in your gowns from Sydney standing in front of the microphone singing those harsh words as if they were nothing more than a pop song. Sing hard, drab little bird, because no matter how hard you sing you'll never sing from your heart the way I sang on those glorious nights. Ripperty! Kye! A-hoo! became my song of joy. I loved those dinners with strangers and being the centre of attention. I thought I was the ants pants, the most talented, most elegant girl in the whole world and the way Mister Bacon's eyes shone with pride when he showed me off only confirmed my uniqueness. After I had finished my poem he would say to his visitor, 'A year or so ago she was just a savage in the jungle.' I'd sit in my chair, which almost swallowed me up it was so big and, chock-full of myself, I'd tell the most outrageous lies about my tribe's savagery and cannibalism. The stories made the visitor marvel even more at my remarkable transformation from a savage primitive into a civilised young lady. I suppose these rare visitors made lurid assumptions about my relationship with Mister Bacon but he obviously didn't care and I had no idea what was in the minds of white men.

Apart from these occasional visitors we spent most of the time in a world of our own. I became his secretary and organised the running of the house. He saw nothing peculiar in a fifteen-year-old native doing this and because I was good at it my role was never questioned. I grew very cocky and lorded it over the staff, especially Maz whom I had never forgiven for betraying me. I rapidly shut her out of Mister Bacon's world, until she seldom appeared in her former territory of the living and dining rooms. Mister Bacon's regular driver was demoted and I became chauffeur when we toured the plantation in his battered Land Rover. To me it was the most majestic car ever made and I felt like a queen as we drove slowly along the tracks between the coffee bushes, my face barely peeking over the dashboard even though I sat on three cushions.

For some time there had been problems with the transportation of the coffee to the coast and so one day Mister Bacon told me to pick two of my favourite dresses, as we were going to the capital in his old prospecting plane. Of course I had never flown before and I had no idea what it would be like. We crammed into the head of the plane and one of the workers spun the propeller. A noise exploded around us like the sound of thunder and screaming birds. My composure shattered. I looked to Mister Bacon for comfort but he was busily concentrating on shifting gears and levers. We ran like an animal after prey across the field and then we were lifted up into the air. I shut my eyes and hunched up in my seat. My intestines, my heart and every part of my guts rushed up my chest and squeezed into my neck. The noise was horrific; like a million cockatoos savaging squealing lizards.

Mister Bacon wanted me to open my eyes but I refused to. It was getting worse. The plane shook as if it were having a fit. Then, as if the agony of rising into the sky were too much, the plane began to fall like a stone. Then it changed its mind and decided to rise again. I felt sick. 'Come on, Palu,' shouted Mister Bacon over the noise, 'have a look!' I peeked through the fingers which covered my eyes and saw nothing. Nothing! Bewildered I sat up and looked out my window. The ground was far below. It was like a dirty tablecloth. I had never imagined everything would look so tiny. I made out a river winding its way like a brown snake through the green forests. It would take days to paddle down it and yet we were doing it in minutes.

There are no words to express my astonishment at this realisation of just how high we were and how fast we were going. I looked ahead and saw a large white cloud. I thought Mister Bacon would fly around it, but instead he headed right for it. Didn't he know what he was doing? Clouds are where the Sky People live. I cried out in alarm. Mister Bacon laughed and we headed into the Sky People's white, misty land. I expected the plane to be ripped apart because of their anger at this intrusion. How would Mister Bacon like it if someone came unannounced in a noisy car and drove through his house! I looked around for the Sky People because I remembered that Sky People look after people when they die. Maybe my mother and father were there. 'Mummy! Daddy!', I shouted into the white world. 'Are you there? Is this the cloud where you live?' There was no answer. Maybe they were living in another cloud. I searched the sky for more clouds for Mister Bacon to drive through but the sky was empty.

Mister Bacon, fearing I had become hysterical, stroked my arm and told me everything was all right. It was the first time he had ever touched me affectionately. 'Enjoy it, Palu,' he yelled over the noise as we left the world of the Sky People and headed into the blue. I gradually calmed down and began to feel like a bird as we drifted over jungles and mountains. I remembered what my father and I had done to the birds of paradise and I felt guilty because I had deprived those creatures of the most wonderul of all sensations: flying. See, there I go, I am squeezing through the bars and I am going to drop a giant turd on your palace and I am remembering the tingling sensation of where Mister Bacon's hand touched me and I am singing 'Ripperty! Kye! A-hoo!' My heart is feeling light as air because I am up here among the Sky People and I can sense my mother and father, even though I cannot see them. 'Ripperty! Kye! A-hoo!'

Then, before I had a chance to get bored, we began to float towards earth like a hawk gliding towards its nest and there, looming up before us, was the biggest village I had ever seen. The roofs were red, the roads were black and grubby brown and stretched as far as the eye could see, and, in the distance, was something I had never seen before: *the sea*! I tried to take all this in but we dropped too quickly. The houses and roads rapidly grew larger and then we dipped and headed towards a large road standing by itself in the middle of a field. I closed my eyes, fearing we would crash, believing that the sky people were throwing us onto the ground for having invaded their territory. A couple of bumps and then silence. A soft hand touches me and a gentle voice says, 'Palu, open your eyes... we're here.'

Port Andrews had about forty thousand people. There were a few white man's mansions and general office blocks but most of the houses were run down and some were merely sheds or shacks. Of course I had seen pictures of cities like Sydney or New York but because I had never experienced anything remotely like those cities they remained merely dreams of some fantastic imagination. The noise, the hustle and bustle and electric lights of Port Andrews made me feel as if I were in a gigantic metropolis. I was so entranced by it all that Mister Bacon had to pull me out of the way of cars several times. I waited for him in the various places he had to go and then in the afternoon he took me to a shop where he bought me a dozen dresses and shoes to match. He got my ears pierced and bought me shiny earrings. That night he took me to a business colleague's house for dinner. How naive I must have been then. I did not realise that those fixed smiles were used to hide their dismay at my presence (and disgust at Mister Bacon's fall from white man's standards) and that their lapsing into simple, short sentences was an act of condescension towards me and not friendly small talk. Mister Bacon took no notice of their attitudes. What people thought of him no longer mattered to him and probably had not done so for years. I thought that the husband and wife regarded me as wonderfully literate and quite, quite beautiful as we sipped drinks before dinner (my first lemonade, the beginning of my addiction to it). How can I concentrate when there is that fraudulent girl on the radio? Why doesn't one of the guards turn her off?

They're too cowardly because they know that the first man to stop her singing is a dead man.

Then, without warning, a girl, their daughter, appeared: an extraordinary, radiant girl of my age. She was wearing a frock almost like mine and I knew instantly (the moment still strikes me to the core of my soul) that *she* was the attractive one. Her pale, smooth skin matched the white dress perfectly. She wore lipstick and make-up, like the models I had seen in magazines — her lips looked like they were stained with betel nut juice and her eyelids were dyed a pale grass colour. Her long ginger hair flowed around and down her shoulders. She looked like one of the beautiful fairy princess dolls I cuddled at night. And it struck me that *I* was the fraud. My short curly hair, black skin that could show no make-up, thick nose and lips were hideous. With the awful realisation of how ugly I was came an even greater sense of horror — I must seem to her to be an embarrassing and pathetic parody of European ideals of beauty. The girl tried to be nice to me as a Western upbringing had taught her to be (why don't you sneer at me so I can jump on you and claw your face, tear your dress, *blacken* you with bruises). Throughout dinner I felt dead as if my brain had dissolved and all that was left was this silly golliwog fumbling with cutlery and choking on fish bones. Mister Bacon noticed my dark mood and I told him I wasn't feeling well. Before I knew what was happening he had whisked me back to the hotel where we were staying. I protested that I didn't want to destroy his evening and that he should return to dinner. 'They bored me rotten,' he smiled. 'All I needed was an excuse to get out of there.'

He put me to bed, thinking I was physically ill. My world was destroyed. My soul was desolated. I knew myself to be comic, ugly and stupid. To comfort me Mister Bacon kissed me goodnight before heading off to his room. The kiss was like that of a father to his daughter. It broke down my defences. I began to cry. He asked what was the matter but I could not stop the flood. After a time I had recovered enough to be able to pour out my despair to him. He said all the right things; no, I was not comic, pathetic, ugly or stupid. On the contrary he found me intelligent and very pretty. He held me in his arms for what seemed hours. Although distraught I found his tenderness overwhelming. No one had ever held me close like that, not even my mother. I wanted to be in his arms forever. I told him I loved him and how much I feared being separated from him. Unknowingly I spoke to him like a lover. You see, I did not know what had been in my heart but when I heard myself say I loved him I realised it was true. Sometimes you must hear yourself speak in order to know what you feel. I pleaded with him to stay and comfort me for the rest of the night. Poor Mister Bacon, what chance did he have? My words had woken in him something that he, too, had hidden from himself. We made love. As he kissed me down my neck and licked my breasts I felt an intense joy I had never experienced before. Wauru and I had barely touched, we had been animals on heat. Mister Bacon was different, even in the way he made love — the missionary position, which meant that I could stare at him. After it was over he fell asleep beside me. I watched him for a long time, feeling exquisite happiness. I felt like a woman for the first time. I realised, as he lay there, his face sprayed with the moving shadows of the palm tree outside the window, that he must have been attracted to me for some time but had kept it hidden, even to himself, believing his actions were merely a gesture to bring civilisation to a savage. Next morning he told me we wouldn't be making love again as it was wrong but the following night, back at the plantation, I went to his bed, unable to sleep without him. We became lovers. Right now, on this becalmed night, with the disturbed voices of scared prisoners in nearby cells enveloping me, I can still feel the quiet, soft flesh of this old man as he held me after we first made love. It amused me that I once considered him a bat demon. When I told him this he laughed, 'Thank God, Palu, that you've given up your silly superstitions.' I might not believe he was a bat demon anymore, but I was still very much part of a world of beliefs and superstitions that I could never tell him about.

Is that me? Was that really me sitting opposite this sixty-year old plantation owner at dinner, as if we were husband and wife? Was it true that I was his lover and that his old penis was inside my young vagina? It seems centuries ago, as if it really wasn't me but some distant ancestor. A few moments ago I heard shots. It sounds as if a new round of executions has started. Now I understand why those prisoners were crying and whispering so feverishly. I know I must hurry if I am to finish telling you about myself to stop his lies. No, I did not give birth to deformed children during my union with Mister Bacon. No, there is no hideous creature in the valley, a son of mine who is part human, part dog. No, Mister Bacon did not rape me or I seduce him with witches' potions. We were in love, two lonely exiles in a curious but true love. And no, I did not kill him. The truth is more simple. I found him in the shower, his body curled up in the corner like a wrinkled foetus, the water raining on his dead face. He had died of a heart attack. I was sixteen and crazy with grief.

Two days after Mister Bacon died his daughter, Irene, and her husband arrived from Australia. She was thin and cold like the pictures of her mother, and she was as imperious as her father had said she would turn out to be. Her loathing of her father's relationship with me was made worse by the fact that I was wearing one of her dresses and yet I was not ashamed of doing so. I took her down into the cellar where I had laid out Mister Bacon on an old table and covered him with orchids and branches of coffee cherries. She gasped as if confronted by some obscene, primitive ceremony, 'Why have you brought him down here and done this to him?'

I explained that as it was the coolest room in the house it would stop him from rotting too quickly and that I had put the flowers on him because that is what you do to the corpse of a great chief. It had taken me the whole day to collect the orchids and I had sat beside him on both nights, keeping a vigil and singing 'Ripperty! Kye! A-hoo!' to remind him of our happy times together and to stop myself from screaming out at my loss. Irene lifted a handful of the orchids from his face and stared at him, trying to feel grief but there was none for a father who had been merely a shadow in her life.

She spent the rest of the day going through her father's papers until she eventually found his will, giving her the plantation if her mother died. Irene decided to sell the plantation as quickly as possible so that there would be no reminders left of a childhood spent in this hated country.

At dinner we ate in silence. Her husband, a bank manager, was lost in this alien world while Irene was most uncomfortable in the role of having to treat the black mistress of the house as her equal. It took all my courage to speak to this awful woman and when I finally did, I asked her if Mister Bacon could be buried on the plantation as it was one of his dearest wishes. She agreed and after she and her husband had flown out next morning, I had Mister Bacon buried by the river. The sight of him vanishing into the red soil deranged me. Again I had lost someone close to me, someone who was my father, lover, protector and teacher. I had paid full price again for my breaking of the taboo. Grief-stricken I tore off my white dress and rolled naked on the warm, moist earth of his grave, covering my face with the soil. I called out his name, wanting to die with him. Guilty at living while he was dead I rubbed a rough wad of leaves and nettles into my cunt until I bled. I screamed out his name for hours until I lost my voice.

A few days later Mr Doyle, a business acquaintance of Mister Bacon's, arrived from Port Andrews to oversee the selling of the property. Only when he arrived did I realise how precarious was my position. With my lover dead I had no right to even live in the house. I would have to return to being a barefoot servant in the house where I had been mistress. What else was there for me? I could not return to tribal ways but nor could I stand the humiliation of being a servant in the house I had run. Mr Doyle asked me what I was going to do. I said I didn't know. 'You're intelligent, Palu. You speak excellent English, why don't you teach your own people? The Australian government wants to give this country independence as soon as possible but it's worried that the people won't be educated enough to run themselves. There's a teachers' college in Port Andrews, why don't you learn to teach? I can recommend you. The government's so desperate for teachers that you'll be paid to learn.'

The next day I flew out with Mr Doyle, taking with me my best dresses, *Gulliver's Travels*, some novels by Dickens and a photograph of Mister Bacon and I sitting on the front veranda being served cold drinks by Maz. I am sure that to others who saw the photograph we looked a queer couple, but what to these people was a sign of Mister Bacon's lonely madness was to he and I paradise. As the plane left the ground I looked back at the receding plantation, realising I had been cast out of Paradise twice. We flew through a stormy, cloudy sky. The Sky People, annoyed at us for disturbing them, tossed the plane around as if they were playing ball. I wasn't afraid because I felt Mister Bacon's spirit amid the clouds protecting us, and he was whispering to me *Palu, I am here, all around you, I'll keep you safe. I am here and in the ground and all around you.*

There is a screaming in the air and the smell of death is all around, even the guards are nervous. They pace the corridor like animals who can smell the blood of the slaughterhouse and fear that they, too, will be next. There is a whistling spinning like a willy-willy through the cells. Tomorrow morning the river will redden with blood and the fat crocodiles will grow fatter. I, too, am scared and the pencil shakes as I write these words. I pray that the guard will arrive soon and fuck away my fear. The gecko's eyes are luminous red, reflecting the fire burning the belongings of the executed outside my window. The gecko looks like those paintings of the angel of death on Christian church walls. The slaughter is changing you, dear gecko, please, please, turn away from the window, do not become entranced by the killings. Look to me. Go *tsk, tsk.* We need each other because we share the same destiny.

The guard did come to my cell. It is good, I thought, that we do not fuck in the missionary position, for our eyes would reflect, like two mirrors, our dread and fear. It is good to be doing the most intimate act in such a way that one can be selfishly caught up in one's own passion. The love making gave me some momentary relief. As I lay on the floor watching him do up his trousers I caught him staring at me and I saw him thinking *yes, she is a witch, she does deserve to die. She has enchanted the President and she is causing this nightmare.* Then I saw another thought enter him *she is calm now, even calmer than me. She gets pleasure out of this.* And then it occurred to him, the thought that disturbs all males *she is using me. I am not using her. She is taking me, swallowing me. Enchanting me.* He had wanted me to look at him with the eyes of hate but I only expressed relief. He went to the door, paused and cursed me. I looked up at my gecko. His eyes are clear and black now. He is guarding me, allowing me to sleep, so no evil spirit will take me tonight.

The teachers' college was a centre of well-intentioned madness. Because independence was rushing upon us and had been badly prepared for, the government was attempting to churn out as many indigenous teachers and public servants as possible. Students for the college had been drawn from all over the country, from missionary schools and village schools, and then been suddenly plonked on the outskirts of Port Andrews and told to become teachers. I was amazed to think that after two years these poor, confused creatures would be sent off to strange places to start schools and teach people whose way of life had not altered in ten thousand years. Everyone was bewildered, including our instructors from Australia, who found that not only did many of the students not understand other students' languages but that the only sort of English they knew was pidgin, a language the whites had not learnt. Only a few students, including myself, spoke English and the teachers were so grateful for this that we soon became teachers' pets.

I was astonished at first, too. I never knew our country had so many languages, so many different tribes. One of the most extraordinary things was that we weren't all black. Our skins ranged from light brown to night black. The light brown skin was characteristic of the coastal tribes but as the tribes went further inland their skins grew darker until, from the distant, recently explored north-west, came reports of people so black that even the whites of their eyes were grey. These Night People lived at night and slept during the day. It was noticeable that not only the skin changed colour as one moved inland but also the body itself. The brown men of the coast were almost Western looking but as the tribes went further inland so the lips grew thicker, the nose broader and flatter and the eyes more deeply set as if blackness had deformed the body itself. My looks were those of someone halfway between the coastal tribes and the Night People. How I wished I had been born on the coast. The boys and girls were so beautiful, lithe and Western looking.

All these different languages and skins made me aware that I was living in a much larger and more diverse country than I had ever thought possible. Most of us were solitary representatives of our tribal areas and so we were forced to get to know people we wouldn't have ordinarily known. Those who did come from the same tribal areas banded together, as tribes will, and fights frequently broke out between these gangs. Most of these fights were caused by boys trying to be tough but we girls got on well together because there were only twelve of us. We slept apart from the boys in a large corrugated shed on disposal store army beds. Although the girls talked about how pretty the coastal boys were there was no hanky panky because most of the girls had been educated by missionaries and taught to regard sex before marriage as a sin. The girls had heard rumours about Mister Bacon and I and did not know what to make of one who had committed sin so young. Yet they were envious of me because I had been the mistress of a rich white man.

In these early days at college I was a real skite and show off. My English was better than anyone else's and while the other girls wore cheap general store cotton dresses and thongs, I wore high heels and the dresses Mister Bacon had bought for me. Oh, Mr Gecko, picture me then, dressed to the nines, sticking out like a sore thumb, amid shorts, thongs and tee shirts. I even corrected the English of my teachers! You're laughing; what a strange, hoarse laugh you've got. I'm laughing too because there is my seventeen-year-old self flouncing from class to class, always a thick novel under her arm and a bored look on her face as if she's surrounded by morons. She's five foot nothing in height and her swelled head is six foot everything. By mastering English I had become Princess of the Plantation, now I thought I was Queen of my Peers.

My English and my appearance attracted the attention of the boys and I often saw them looking at me with that male mixture of envy and hate which I had also seen in the eyes of the plantation workers. The boys, however, didn't interest me. I still had Mister Bacon. At night, while the other girls slept, he came to me and held me in his arms. He talked to me gently, softly of his boyhood in Australia, of his search for gold and his coffee bean plantation. We made love until piccaninny daylight and then he would go, vanishing into the dawn sunlight, leaving behind his smells and semen. Some nights he would be annoyed with me for some reason or another and I would have to call him, whispering so the other girls didn't hear me *Mister Bacon, come to me. I am lonely. I want you.* And, after a time, I would detect the aroma of coffee beans and he would appear at my bedside, his blue eyes shining and his white hair glowing. As the year went on it became more difficult to summon him up until one night he did not come at all. When he did come the following night it was only after hours of pleading with him. He did not come to bed but stood near the doorway, his eyes vague and his hair grey and lifeless. He was like a wooden statue I once saw dragged out of a river which had been in the water so long that it had been worn smooth, so smooth that it was not known if it were a man or a woman or a god. As he stood gazing at me I realised he would never come to me again. Some nights I heard him weeping from under the earth where he was buried but there was nothing I could do to help him. Sometimes there was so much anguish in his weeping that I had to cover my ears so as not to hear him, just as now I am loudly dictating to myself to stop myself from hearing the weeping coming from outside. Women are wailing on hearing what has happened to their sons, lovers and husbands last night. They cry out 'We want to be fed to the crocodiles too. We want to die too!' Can you hear the weeping as you try to sleep? Is the sound of their weeping whirling through the palace corridors looking for you? Or are you covering your ears as I did when Mister Bacon wept? I will tell everyone straight, no bullshit, why that lonely old man wept in his grave by the river; because he knew, even before I did, that I was forgetting him. I didn't even realise myself how preoccupied I was becoming with another man.

It all started out of jealousy. I have told you how full of myself I had become and how I adored being the centre of attention, especially with the teaching staff. However, as the year went on, I saw that another student, a boy, was becoming the favourite of teachers who had always seen me as their favourite. Was I put out! At first I even denied to myself that I was jealous and I could not understand why I became irritated every time the girls mentioned this boy's name. 'Don't be silly,' I said to them when they called him a spunk, 'you really are little girls. Can't you think of anything more elevated than boys!' I don't think I was attracted to him then, I was merely jealous of the way teachers saw him as someone *special*. I was supposed to be the *special* one!

This boy from the coast had the greatest lust for Western knowledge I had ever seen. It was such a lust that it was a sickness. It consumed him, possessed him like a fever. Oh, yes, I recognised my own lust in that boy, but whereas I devoured works of the imagination, his hunger was for facts and theories. Bored by literature classes, he came alive during social studies or science. One particular teacher, a brown-bearded man with a large nose and permanent frown, called Mr Andrews, took a great interest in this student of his and I would often see them talking after class or meandering together through the college garden, yapping about something that was being deliberately denied to me. He gave this boy books to read and topics to think about. Why didn't Mr Andrews treat me like that? I sulked and became increasingly irritated, making smart-arsed comments in Mr Andrews' social studies classes. This boy's English was not as good as mine and to prove I was better at the subject I would show off in English classes. I didn't care that the teacher tried to shut me up or rolled her eyes in exasperation as I answered all the questions. All I cared about was being top of the class. One time this boy answered a question by saying 'I think he were' and I laughed loudly at his mistake and mockingly corrected him. He looked at me angrily but I pretended I didn't notice. Later on in a maths class he got his revenge by publicly correcting my algebra. I was furious. The class laughed. Afterwards I found myself seething with anger. I wanted to hit him or verbally beat him into submission. Why didn't I go and talk to him then? If I approached him first then that would mean he had defeated me. No, he had to approach me first. So there is stuck-up Palu sitting on the grass pretending to read *Dombey & Son* while, all the time, her ears are pricked and her eyes are secretly on Mr Andrews talking to this boy near the tree of flaming red flowers. What is so engrossing to them? I don't care what you are talking about, I think, and yet I am straining to hear the words. I hate being left out.

Then there is another time. Forty of us are in a classroom before the teacher arrives, gossiping about one of the girls who has a spider (it entered through her belly button) living in her stomach, tormenting her with bad dreams and awful menstruation pains. There is a question put: Should we bring in a sorcerer to get rid of the spider? This must be done secretly because the whites will laugh at us if they find out. I am saying we should get a sorcerer as soon as possible when suddenly I am interrupted. It's that boy again! He pushes his way through the group and takes over the platform. He looks at me angrily, as he does at the rest of the students. 'You are all stupid to believe such stories,' he says, admonishing us and then, before we can reply, he storms out of the classroom. I want to kill him. I hate him for his air of arrogant superiority. You don't know anything about these important matters! The next day I was proved right when the sorcerer came and pulled a giant red and blue spider from out of the girl's vagina. Did you acknowledge that I was right? No, you looked away. I thought I had conquered you by having been seen publicly to be right but something has happened; you have taken over my mind like the spider taking over the girl's body. I cannot stop thinking about you, so much so that even if Mister Bacon were weeping I would not hear him.

At the end of the year we had a big party to celebrate the fact that everyone had passed first year (although some of us rightly suspected that the government had demanded that no one fail because it needed the teachers so badly). We took over one of the tin sheds, dancing to rock'n'roll and drinking beer. Soon we were all bathed in sweat. My best dress, a pale sky blue frock, had started off frilly and pert but quickly began to droop and hang limply, even the orchids in my hair wilted. I was in a strange state of excitement and didn't know why. Maybe it was because the year had finished or the fact that all the boys wanted to dance with me. When your eyes, dear gecko, capture the morning sun, they seem on fire and so my eyes must have looked similarly aflame that night. I couldn't sit still but danced as if possessed by some unknown passion.

After dancing with a stupidly handsome fellow from one of the islands I went to the bucket for some beer and as I did so, my eyes caught someone else's. It was him, staring at me from the other side of the room, through the writhing, twisting dancers. He held my gaze contemptuously. Standing alone and aloof, drinking his beer, it was as if he were saying *I do not like this but I will drink and be here if everyone thinks it is so important*. I hated the way he was looking down on us all, as if we were primitive and uncouth. I wanted to scratch his face and tear at his eyes. I hurried through the dancers and confronted him. 'Who do you think you are, smarty-pants?!'

What a terribly clever comment I had made! I was so livid that I resorted to using obscenities from my own language and although he didn't understand my words I called him dog-shit, boy lover and old vagina. As I abused him he smiled. That smile! It struck me to the core. It was the smile of victory. I was the one who had approached him! I had lost. I wanted to bite him, scratch him, punch him. Then, without a word, he walked away. I called out after him, 'Where are you going?' He pointed outside. Angry and wanting to attack him, I followed him. Going through the doorway I was hit by the cool sea air and it struck me how suffocating and hot it was inside the tin shed. There he was, ahead of me, pretending I didn't exist, walking to the knoll at the end of the college garden which overlooked Port Andrews and the sea. Still furious, but made a bit calmer by the cool night air, I ran after him.

'You think you're so superior to everyone!'

He turned and smiled at me. 'But you think you are too.'

His answer stopped me. It was true, I did think I was superior, but nobody had ever told me to my face. I was shocked that anybody could and I found myself unable to reply. I stood before him, my sweaty dress drying on my skin, hearing, as if in a distant dream, the raucous music coming from the shed. Not knowing what to do or say I looked away and saw flying foxes, fat with fruit, loping slowly across the face of the full moon on their way back home. Everything seemed quiet as if it were spellbound by the night. All the anger left me as did the triumphant smile on his face. We looked at each other silently and I realised what I had hidden from myself; the girls were right, he was a truly beautiful man. Caught in the moonlight his pale skin was like copper. His face was soft, like a Westerner's, not like a Highlander's face which seem as if they are harshly put together by an irritated sculptor. I felt my chest constricting as if held in an enormous vice. Dear gecko, I was like a night animal bedazzled by a torchlight. How can I explain the change in me? His presence was so powerful and he was so handsome that I felt helpless. I wanted him to engulf me, swallow me up. Instead he turned away to look at the sea.

'You been to Australia?' he asked softly. I moved up beside him, too scared to look directly at him for fear of revealing just how vulnerable I was and followed his gaze out across the black ocean with its highway of white light leading from the horizon to the shore.

'No.'

'Then that Australian never took you there?'

'No.'

My answer seemed to satisfy him for the moment but I knew he wanted to know more, as everyone did, about my relationship with Mister Bacon. I had realised since being in Port Andrews that Mister Bacon was a legend in my country. He was the bird man who had brought coffee to the backlands.

'Would you like to go to Australia?'

'Wouldn't everyone?'

He nodded in agreement. He envied me for my association with Mister Bacon because I had become close to a rich white and whites had and knew everything. Realising he was jealous of me made him seem less conceited and more human. He stood with his eyes averted, gazing at the sea, his hands in the pockets of his shorts and his shirt open, exposing his handsome chest. Just as I am desperate to touch you, gecko, so I can feel your beating heart that is tantalisingly visible, and therefore vulnerable, so I wanted to feel his smooth, muscular coppery skin. Shy, for one of the first times in my life, I could think of nothing to say in the long silence.

Do men realise the power they have over women at these moments? Finally he took a cigarette out of his pocket and lit it, 'It's my last one so we'll have to share it.'

We smoked it slowly, in silence, passing it back and forth. He with his eyes on the sea, me with my eyes on him. We were almost within touching distance. I wanted him to accidentally touch me when he passed the cigarette. I had never felt the desire to be touched so strongly before. Even now I am astonished at the complete turnabout in my attitude to him. Perhaps it was magic. I'm sure that had something to do with it because later he told me that he had placed one of his pubic hairs in the cigarette to cast a spell of love over me.

When we were down to the butt he flicked it away and then, almost as if a command had been given, he turned to me and I leaned forward to him. When he touched my arm the whole of my body tingled. He was open-mouthed with lust and so was I. He slowly rubbed his face against mine, his stubbled cheeks causing prickles of excitement to run through my body. I rubbed my cheeks against his, pressing them into the bones of his face. Our frenzy grew and we rubbed our faces hard against each other, faster and more violently, rubbing so hard that I could feel blood emerging from my chaffed skin and mingling with his. We rubbed cheeks and bit off each other's eyelashes until we were exhausted and then, with our faces smeared with blood and puffy with lust we made love. After it was over I would not let him out of me. The whole world was impregnated with blood, sperm, love and ripeness. I kissed his bloody face and he told me that he had secretly desired me from the first day he saw me. I had to acknowledge to myself that if I didn't know I had wanted him, my spirit had. In the distance the rock'n'roll music continued but we lay in a lovers' silence. Wrapped in his arms I knew I never wanted to be apart from him and could only utter the diminutive of his name as if it were a magic incantation: 'Emo, Emo, Emo...'

It was impossible to pry us apart for the next few weeks. I had no eyelashes left and my face was a permanently tingling rash. Most of the students had returned to their villages for the vacation and so we had the college to ourselves. We made love everywhere; in the girls' dorm, in the boys' dorm, in the gardens, under the sago trees. One time we sneaked into a college house and made love on the clean white sheets of a teacher who had returned to Australia for a few weeks. Emo looked so beautiful when he lay on that bed, like a glistening black starfish on a white beach and when he opened his mouth to laugh it was as pink as a lotus flower. In order to be more attractive to him I would sneak off in the morning and roll on the dewy lawns, speaking words of love to his sleeping spirit and then I would rub aromatic plants over my body. When I returned to bed we would feed each other bananas and pandanus fruit or if we had been to the market we would have juicy sago grubs. I loved Mister Bacon like a father, I loved Emo like a lover.

We took long walks to the capital and sniggered at the gawking hicks wearing nothing but lap-laps and arse grass. We looked down on them because they chewed betel nut and spat out its juice indiscriminately, so that the muddy footpaths were splattered with it as if a thousand bleeding men had passed by. On the way back to college Emo liked to stop and look at the Catholic Church. I asked him what was so special about it and he pointed to a large wooden angel perched above the doorway. 'What do you think of angels?' he asked. I laughed and said I didn't believe in them.

'But you have your superstitions, Palu. You believe in demons, ghosts and spiders in girls' stomachs.'

'But they're real, angels aren't.'

'Oh, Miss Big Head is back,' he teased.

Later that night as we lay in the dark after making love, he was quiet for a long time as if thinking deeply about something. I had my head on his chest, listening to his heart. 'You're lucky, Palu,' he finally said.

'Why?'

'Your parents are gone and you have been thrown out of your tribe.'

I laughed, thinking he was being funny.

'No, I mean it. Tribes place so many obligations on you. It's so hard to break free of them.' He then told me he had to return to his tribe for a week because his sister was marrying. He couldn't take me because I was an outsider, someone from the hated Highlands. He detested such tribal loyalties because they bound him to a past he wanted to forget and yet he had to go. Once he was gone I wandered the college and Port Andrews like a lost soul. It was as if a sorcerer had taken my spirit. I had no concentration at all. I would start to read and then find my attention wandering after only a page. My whole mind was filled with Emo. He possessed it utterly. I thought of crazy things; of following him to his village or of drowning myself if he didn't return. At night I sat on the knoll where we had first made love and I talked to his spirit, telling him how much I loved him. A week later he still had not returned and I became frantic and could not sleep. Late that night he silently appeared in the doorway of the girls' dormitory. I exploded with joy. I hugged and kissed him and, randy as hell, I ran up and down the shed, jumping from empty bed to empty bed like a drunken demon, crying out, 'Palu loves Emo!' Other people would have thought I was mad, but Emo didn't. He was as besotted with me as I was with him. How can I tell you, gecko, how happy I was that night. I was like those cowboys in a Hollywood movie I once saw who got drunk, took out their six guns and rode up and down the main street of the town, hollering and laughing and shooting the sky.

The new prison governor has been chosen well. He is a real blockhead from the backlands; black as night, stupid and obedient. He even has your picture on the wall. Is that why the other governor was gotten rid of; because he didn't have your picture in his office? Today was the governor's first day and because I am prize exhibit, I was taken to him. On the way across the compound my nostrils were filled with the stench from the river. Even the crocodiles are too full to eat anymore and corpses float, unmolested, down the river like rafts of flesh carrying lazy river birds. Was the new governor appalled by his promotion to this abattoir? Of course not; see his bearing, his preening. Look at me he's saying *I'm cock of the walk, I am here because the President himself has promoted me and I am meeting Mrs President.*

After being brought before him he had me stand in front of his desk while he ostentatiously went through my file as if never having read it when, in fact, he knew it by heart. 'Now, let's see, how long have you been here, two months, eh?' While he pretended to be engrossed in my file I looked at your photograph. It's a new one; there's no smile. Your eyes have been dulled so that it's harder for people to tell what you're thinking and the wrinkles have been smoothed away but even the inept retoucher cannot make you unhandsome. I wish you were ugly and fat like the governor but you still have your beauty and masculine charm, things that always astonish the women reporters from the West as if they somehow expected you to be an ugly demon. Instead they are bowled over by you. I grew tired of you enchanting them. That smile which you had not bestowed on me for some time was freely given to those simpering white ghosts who could not hide the thought *I want to make love to him.* They came to talk to you about your dictatorship and returned to their democracies, gushing about your charismatic presence. Did they come to me to ask my opinions about you? Western women journalists are not interested in the wife, for all their talk to the contrary they are fascinated by powerful men. And they are fascinated by you, you who are so handsome in your Western suits.

That image on the wall, I imagine your fat toady prays to it. He thinks you are god incarnate and I am a witch. How long has he been out of the backlands? Not long, just enough to learn a bit of English for official occasions and when he's with the boys he lapses back into pidgin. He has found himself with more power over people than he ever imagined. While he was still going through my file I asked him *the* question, 'How long before my husband has me executed?' The question jolted him. He had never heard the President referred to as *husband*. It is so shockingly familiar. The word also shakes him because it reminds him of the delicacy of his situation. He knows that the President wants his wife executed but that is now and what if it could be that he changes his mind; you know how tricky, notoriously tricky, husband and wife relationships can be. The President might change his mind and want her back and what will happen then? She'll start talking about how the prison governor... He pondered his position, looking at me with the eyes of a confused animal. I am definitely not going to be as easy a case as he thought.

'I do not know if you are going to be executed, Mrs...'

He was going to say 'Mrs President' but is bewildered as to just the right term to use. I played this wrongly. He hates me now because I have brought confusion and difficulty into a job he thought was going to be a piece of cake. Sometimes I can be such a smart arse. I should have been more astute. All he wanted was to have a long rambling talk with me and impress me with his godlike powers, instead, he found himself wanting me out of his office as soon as possible. He had meant to be stern with me but knew he couldn't. I am a much too delicate situation for a man who has lived by coarse decisions.

'Any complaints,' he asked, not wanting to hear any.

I shook my head and he nodded to the guard to return me to my cell. I glanced one last time at you and was immediately possessed by doubt; I want to hate you but so far I've learnt only to hate the President.

Walking back across the compound it began to rain. For a while at least the rain will wash away the stench. Looking at the brick and wooden buildings it was hard to imagine that this prison did not exist four years ago. It seems so permanent and full of purpose now. The prisoners have cut back the jungle so that now we seem trapped on some monstrous, barren island. Sometimes I think it was not the prisoners who pushed back the jungle at all but the jungle which, finding the prison so terrible, retreated of its own will.

It occurred to me, once back in my cell, that those eyes which I consider dead are, to others, glazed with power, as if they are two brown sacs of the most indescribably potent magic. People don't expect to see *your* eyes glowing with spirit; powerful men must keep their inner power hidden. Remember when you showed me some books you had about twentieth century leaders. You admired the pictures of men like Lenin and Mao, men who had radically transformed their country. Their eyes, did you notice their eyes? They were like the eyes of cooked fish. Were their eyes once like yours; full of life and fire? It is strange to be thinking these thoughts but the photograph of you and the meeting with the new governor has unnerved me. Does the appointment of this new governor mean my death is imminent? I always imagined that the signs of my approaching execution would be more obvious. But what exactly would be the signs? Your personal arrival to witness my execution would be an act of love or hate and I don't think you feel those emotions anymore.

I want my guard. I am starting to tremble. Come to me and screw me into an insensible sleep. He has stayed away for two days. I know he is out there because I can hear him walking up and down the corridor. For a heavy set man he is surprisingly light on his feet. He does not enter my cell because he is still angry with me for using him. Like the governor, my guard is one of the Night People. My husband has reached into the darkest corner of the country to find his guards and killers. Who would have thought that this cinnamon-skinned man would turn away from his own kind and employ these Night People as his servants. After thousands of years of being regarded as the lowliest of all tribes these Blacks are now enjoying lording it over anyone who is lighter. My guard is a typical Night Man; fat lips, squat, broad nose and deep set eyes like grey windows in a black house. Like most of us have or will be he is straddling the abyss of thousands of years.

*

70

Like Emo and I. We were both trying to jump the abyss as quickly as possible. I was not interested in sociology and politics, just as he was not interested in my novels. We took our separate interests for granted as we hungrily devoured the West, lying side by side, books in our hands after making love so passionately that for hours afterwards I thought I was only a part of myself. One afternoon we had been so energetic making love that when we finished I saw that a few comics had emerged from under the bed. I picked them up and saw they were *Phantom* comics. 'You read these?' I teased. Embarrassed he snatched them from my hand and threw them back under the bed. He soon retrieved them, however, and said sheepishly 'Do you want me to read them to you?' I said yes and so he read one about the Phantom saving a girl from the clutches of a mad King in the jungle. Emo adored the Phantom, admiring his heroism and the way he and his dog, Devil, rid the world of evil. When he read me the stories of 'The Ghost Who Walks', he would get caught up with the adventures, even though he had read them many times before, and like a child becoming engrossed, would stop reading aloud and continue to read on silently, forgetting he had a listener. *The Phantom* comics were the one piece of literature we had in common and we often discussed the Phantom as seriously as one would discuss the life of Mao or the adventures of David Copperfield.

Emo's energy devoured me and everyone else. When he played football he would kick the ball so hard with his bare feet that I thought either the ball would burst or his toes break. This same aggression and purpose went into his quest for knowledge. Mr Andrews often invited us to his house and he and Emo would talk and talk and talk. They talked of our country being a colony, a Third World country, and of Australia being an imperialist power. What I found remarkable was that a white man would criticise his own kind. 'We are destroying you,' he would say, 'independence can't come quick enough.' I had never heard anyone criticise their own tribe and because Mr Andrews did I mistrusted him. I was also wary of him because he had a beard. Magicians often have beards so you can't see their faces properly. 'Emoti,' he said, 'you are a man to lead your people eventually. Once independence comes nothing will change. Your people will still ape the white man.' Why, I asked myself, did Mr Andrews give my awed lover books that talked of hatred against the white man? Suspicious of him I watched the spit that formed on his beard. If green spit appeared then it would be certain proof that Mr Andrews was a magician; but it never did. His beard would be spotted with spittle, his shirt and shorts grubby with bread crumbs and mango juice, and still he would not stop talking. I said nothing on such occasions, believing that these conversations were men's talk. Just as men conducted wars back in the villages, so Mr Andrews and Emo spoke of another kind of war. God, that white man could talk. He was forever lecturing Emo on what to read and how to interpret. Emo could barely get a word in edgewise. But then when we got home he would lecture me on Mr Andrews' ideas. Of course I admired my lover for his convictions. I suppose my admiration was made even greater by the fact that I had none myself. Do not smile, dear gecko, I am telling you the truth when I say I had none. Why do you think I have ended up here?

In his desire to have our country become modern, Emo cut himself off from his own past, a past that was full of the irrational; demons, ghosts, absurd myths and stupid ceremonies. He regarded our primitiveness with a real loathing and to illustrate what he called 'our primitive stupidity' he would hold up his left hand and show the only flaws in his body; two deformed fingers. As part of an initiation ceremony when he was a young boy he had been forced to put his hand into the boiling insides of a roasting pig. 'What was the point of that?' he would ask rhetorically and then lecture his most willing audience more. 'You must get rid of *your* superstitions, Palu.' I tried to please him by doing so but I could not erase them from my soul. Emo also tried hard to rise above beliefs he hated. To conquer his fear of menstruation he would sleep with me when I was bleeding but the fear of contamination and impotency was too much and during my periods we did not touch. I did not mind this for I felt contaminated when I was bleeding and had slept apart from Mister Bacon, too, every month. I certainly didn't want Emo to sleep with me during these periods if it was to make him impotent. Our love making was so wonderful that I would have preferred anything to that! When he made love to me I felt as if I lost a part of my self and, strangely, this gave me the feeling that I was whole. It is extraordinary what randiness and love can make you feel. What about you, my bachelor cell mate, do you ever get so randy that nothing else matters or are you just a watcher forever licking your eyes clean of what you have seen?

Emo's determination to oppose tribal laws and beliefs was not to be doubted. His tribe had demanded that once he finish college he marry a woman from a neighbouring tribe as a payback for some obscure incident in the past. He defied this decree by marrying me near the end of our final college year. I was so happy about being married and being able to live with Emo in the converted tool shed the college had given us, that I forgot all about his tribal obligations. Then one night, a few weeks after we were married, I awoke and saw something dark and huge standing in the shed. At first

I thought I was dreaming but as my eyes grew used to the darkness I saw that the figure was a grass demon. Terrified I shook Emo awake. When he saw it he gasped. Grass demons are called up by sorcerers. Part men, part jungle, they are sent out at night to avenge wrongdoing. I grabbed Emo's hand for comfort. His hands were sweating in fear too. The grass demon moved closer, rustling as it walked, sounding like an evil breeze through bamboo. Its face was bright blue and its head was shrouded in leaves and grass that flowed down its neck onto its shoulders like dry witch's hair. The rest of its body was covered in a shroud of bamboo leaves and grass. I had heard of these beasts but had never seen one. I almost shat myself when it jumped forward. It was so close that its leaves touched my feet and sent shivers of fear through me. I could see its eyes and they were looking at me with contempt. Emo started to speak to it. I tried to stop him for fear that his voice might be stolen but he paid no attention. The grass demon replied and I realised that both were speaking the language of Emo's tribe, a language of which I knew very little. Occasionally their voices rose in anger or irritation and the monster would point to me with his leafy fingers. After a time the grass demon's voice grew sad and Emo's more confident and finally it left, disappearing into the night.

To calm ourselves Emo and I smoked until dawn and he told me his tribe had sent the grass demon to threaten him into giving me up. I wondered why the tribe would have sent a grass demon so far to break our marriage and Emo told me he was the chief's grandson. When he told me this I realised I hardly knew anything about him. I had told him all about myself, yet he had told me only of his hopes, his dreams and his love for me. His past was always dismissed as something belonging to that primitive world he despised.

'See,' he said, 'I marry you and it's the crime of a lifetime. They send a fellow dressed in grass to scare me. How stupid can they be. Now do you understand why I hate all of that?'

'But how did you get rid of him, what did you say to him?'

His eyes shone in the dawn light and he smiled mischievously. 'I told him that my life was my own now and if the tribe didn't like it then I would use white man's magic on them. I would come with a gun and kill the sorcerer *and* the grass demon.'

We laughed until we cried but both of us slept restlessly for weeks, waking at any unusual sounds. I wished we had glass or wire in our window to protect us and sometimes I would awake to see a grass demon staring in at us, biding its time before flying in through the window to kill us.

In the past hour or so I have been hearing the guards talking in the corridor. There has been an escape! From what I can figure out someone got away from a work party by changing into a cassowary. The guard saw the cassowary fleeing into the jungle and shot at him but missed. Run cassowary! Run! Someone will have to pay for your bravery, that's for sure. Maybe the whole work party will die. This is the first real test for the new governor. I know what he will do, he will have a tantrum, accuse the guard of being an idiot and then seek revenge.

The taro and sago I have been eating seems bad. My stomach is churning as if it's full of eels. I was thinking of when you laughed in those days; everybody would join in. Your mouth would open like a red fruit, ripening and cracking in the warm sun and from inside a laugh would come bursting out, prolonged and loud as if all the emotions and tensions you kept inside exploded into joy. Those who only know you now will think I am imagining this, but once, my black Phantom, you were truly human. And once you wore shoes for the first time. Look at us then!

Because we were the top of the college we were not sent to the backlands to teach but were given a school in the capital. We were so full of ourselves. We were brilliant. We were *teachers*. We were living in Port Andrews, the capital of the world. Port Andrews, twelve paved roads and the rest turned to mud when it rained. And there you are on your first day at school, nervous as a child, your feet screaming because they're bound in leather for the first time. Prim and proper you looked. Ironed white shirt, white shorts, long white socks and black leather shoes. In the classroom though, your nerves vanished. The students adored you because they saw your eagerness, your desperate desire to drag them into the modern era. By contrast I was hopeless. Confronted by forty odd students I lost my confidence. They were like ferociously hungry chicks squealing out for food, instead of the docile pups I had imagined who would patiently soak up what I had to say. Most of them were unable to speak English and my pidgin was terrible. The children knew I didn't have my heart in the task and, taking advantage of this, became unruly and aggressive. The only way I could cope was to become detached. In those days I had a great ability to drift and dream away my life. If only I could do that now, here, *right now*! Shut out the horror, shut my ears to the distant screams. Someone's guts are being torn from him by a teenage guard. How can I tell his age? Because teenage boys are the most savage of all. Grab a boy before he turns twenty, give him a gun or knife and a bit of authority and then let his natural urges take over. Bark, gecko, make your noises, make them loud and magnificent and banish that human cry. Will you have your Queen of the Night killed that way? Can you hear that man's screams piercing your soul like a drill? Make no mistake, you will hear mine. They will be so loud that your eardrums will burst open, blood will pour from your nose and your brain will curdle like cream rotting in the sun.

My guard has just gone. I called out for a bowl because I have been vomiting up the putrid taro. Like everyone in this row of cells he is unnerved by the public tortures. Still angry with me, he demanded to know where I kept the pages he gave me. I wouldn't tell him. He threatened to tell the governor but I knew he wouldn't because he would be in real trouble if it were found out that he had given me paper and pen. Another guard came in, wondering what the fuss was about. I said I wanted another shit can. He shrugged, thinking *she's a real pain in the arse* and left my guard to sort out the problem. We were alone, and for a long time he said nothing. He watched me as I lay on the floor grimacing with stomach ache. I could not stop the longing growing in his mind. The witch must have looked vulnerable and easy to take. *I am going to crush you* he thought. *I am the one in control. I always go to you. I am just a thing you use for relief. But I will fuck you, you cunt of a witch, into submission.* When he took me I smelt spicy bark in his mouth and I realised that he had always intended to come here and have sex with me. He did it brutally. If I had been an ordinary prisoner he would have spat on me and hit me until I could not walk. I sense you now, back in your bunk. You will have forgotten about eating the bark and think only that you had no intention of having sex with me. *I was drawn there against my will.* Then, as you think about the visit to my cell, a thought will begin to cloud your mind *the witch has enchanted me and has taken my semen again.* A further confirmation that I am a witch will be the black slimy mess I vomited up just before he left me.

Goggle eyes, did you see what happened? You are my witness. I know you are eyeing me, even though it is day. Somewhere in one of the cracks in the wall you are watching over me like an angel, a guardian angel. Have I told you about Emoti's angels? When Mr Andrews first came to our house, it was more a shack than a house, he was astonished to see a large white angel hanging from the ceiling. Plastic, and therefore quite light, it swayed gently over us, protecting our house. Mr Andrews laughed at it, thinking it was a joke. When we didn't laugh he was taken aback.

'You don't believe in the Christian idea of angels, do you, Emoti?'

Emo was defensive and told him it was a sign of his freedom from tribal thinking.

'But, don't you see, this is Western tribal thinking.'

Annoyed at being laughed at Emo said nothing and retreated into a silence so unsettling to his teacher that the topic was never mentioned again.

Emo's love for angels had started in missionary school. He had been bored by school until one day his teacher stuck a picture of heaven on the classroom wall. Fascinated by the figures with wings he asked what they were and was told they were angels. Angels were eternally good creatures who had overcome death. Emo's tribe had no concept of life after death and the idea that one could survive death intrigued him. Yet the angels' most marvellous quality was that they protected people, unlike his own culture where a child was completely vulnerable to the terrors of demons and had no good ghosts to protect the innocent. Emo told me about his love for angels in a moment of drunkenness after having spent a night talking with Mr Andrews. He would never have told me this when sober because he never wanted to appear weak in my eyes. He certainly would never have told Mr Andrews about the angels, even when drunk. He also would never have told this Australian Marxist that of all the books he had given Emoti, his pupil's favourite was Engels' *The Condition of the Working Class, 1844*. One night while he was re-reading it I asked him why he liked it. 'Palu, I never understood what Hell was until I read that book. People lived in such misery. Poverty and starving everywhere.'

'See,' I teased, 'if you had read Dickens like me you would have known.'

'What a stupid, dumb, idiotic thing to say, Palu!' He looked daggers at me. He hates me talking about Dickens because it reminds him of Mister Bacon. It hurts his pride to think that I may have been influenced by another man and a god at that. It was the same with 'Ripperty Kye A-hoo!' Sometimes when I was happy I found myself singing it and if Emo heard me he grew annoyed, thinking I was daydreaming about Mister Bacon when, in fact, it had become just a song of happiness. Why am I talking about happiness? Where the Dickens am I? The bars on my windows are dancing and I am trying to concentrate. I am sneering at Mr Andrews. He did not understand that those angels had helped Emo escape from the bonds of tribal beliefs. He would not have understood either that the reason the Engels book meant so much to Emo was that he could understand it. I don't think the Australian fully realised that all these theories and ideas he was thrusting at his willing pupil lay undigested in his brain, like a wallaby lying undigested in a python. Even the concept of independence was hard to grasp. What would happen afterwards? What did it actually mean? Could our own people govern themselves? Many whites, fearing bloodshed and chaos, were leaving the country. Emo hated the thought that independence would prove that his own people were incapable of governing themselves. It was going to be an emormous leap for us. 'Picture a Stone Age man,' he told me, 'wearing nothing but arse grass, trying to work a computer — that's us.'

Yet such a leap could be made; Emoti had done it. When he had flown into Port Andrews to start college he had been so superstitious that when the plane flew through the mist-shrouded valleys he thought he was in the land of the dead. He was so afraid that he had to bite his tongue to stop from crying out. When he arrived in the capital he knew no one and wore only arse grass. He had brought with him three cassowaries which he was going to sell to pay his way through college. He took the birds to the site of the next day's market. By that time it was night so he tied up the birds and slept. While he slept he dreamt of being educated, of leaving behind his primitive past, of wearing Western clothes and of becoming leader of his country. When he awoke he discovered that one of his birds had been stolen. Another tribesman would have panicked but not Emoti. He waited until the market opened, sold his remaining birds and then went in search of the third cassowary. He spent all day looking for it in the city. He stopped strangers in the street and asked if they had seen the cassowary. He searched for another five days and still no one could help him, yet he did not give up. He had to find the cassowary because he needed the money to get to college and also because he was a proud man and wouldn't give up until he had found the thief. 'I will follow you, bird-stealer,' he promised, 'to the end of the world.' He reasoned that the culprit might belong to one of the tribes that lived on the fringes of the capital so he visited each tribe in turn and only after three weeks did he find a cassowary that looked like his. He told the tribal chief that it was his bird. 'No, it isn't,' said the chief, 'my son bought it in Port Andrews.' The rest of the tribe gathered threateningly around Emoti, as the chief yelled at this stranger who had accused his son of stealing the bird. Emoti stood his ground and said he would prove he wasn't lying. He asked that the bird be let out of its cage. When it was Emoti called to it. The cassowary came directly to him and lay its head against his chest as he spoke to it in its own language. No one had ever seen one of these aggressive birds behave in such a gentle manner. The chief realised that the stranger was right and gave him back his bird. So impressed was the chief with Emoti's persistence that he wanted to make him his son and give him a big feast with forty pigs but Emoti refused because he had to get back to college. When he sold his cassowary he told it, 'Thank you for recognising me but I must sell you so I can understand the world.' The bird wept as Emoti patted it goodbye, then Emoti went off to a store where he bought some shorts, tee shirts and thongs and got rid of his arse grass for the last time. The world awaited him. What am I writing? I look back at what I have written. My words dance and twist into a hundred shapes. This food poisoning is playing with my mind. The story of Emoti and The Three Cassowaries is part of his official myth. In truth he arrived by plane wearing shorts, a tee shirt and thongs that the missionary school had given him and he went to college on a government scholarship like me. It is curious how vulnerable I, too, can be to his myths. So persistent has this cassowary story been that I almost believe it myself. My cell mate is laughing like a drunken old man *tee hee, tee hee, Palu... you really fell for that piece of ripe old shit*. My skin is burning and my mind is floating. The cassowary story is swirling around inside me because I am unable to get rid of cassowaries. They are everywhere. The man who escaped by turning into a cassowary has been recaptured and some of the young guards are mocking the old guard's story of the transformation by dressing up the prisoner in cassowary feathers and tying a stone to his head so that it resembles a casque. They are forcing him to dance like a cassowary. Whirl around, spin, astonish them by becoming a cassowary and then gently lay your head against Emoti's breast.

It is now two days later. I have been in a delirium. I thought the prison guards had brought me to your bedroom. You were dressed in your best suit and lying on the bed while a young Australian girl yodelled country and western songs on a nearby chair. You looked as if you were dying and said, 'Palu, I want you to stop thinking about me — your thoughts are killing me.' You looked so ill that I clutched you to my breast and discovered that you had no heart beat. You were alive but not living. You felt greasy as if made out of pig fat. I pulled away in fear but your red tongue, metres long like a snake, sprang out of your mouth and wrapped itself around my neck. 'I am immortal. I am the ghost who walks. You can't kill me, Palu.' I began to choke but you only laughed and pressed your black, triumphant eyes against mine and chilled me to my very soul.

I couldn't get this delirious vision out of my mind and cried out for help. I think the prison doctor came but I am not sure about this. The vision had told me one thing; he is scared of my thoughts. Does he suspect that I am writing about him? He didn't seem to know where I kept my papers and pen hidden in the dream. He knows how powerful the word can be; it almost destroyed his career before it began. Together with Mr Andrews he wrote an article for the newspaper called *The Carpetbaggers*. Only Emo's name was attached to it and he took the brunt of the criticism. It caused notoriety because it was true. The article said that foreigners came to our country, bled it dry and then disappeared with the money they had stolen from us. It went on to say that at the first sign of difficulty foreign investors fled and that they were threatening to ruin the country if independence didn't go their way. The article caused a real stink. Emo didn't know that as a teacher employed by the government he was forbidden to publicly criticise government policy. As punishment he was suspended from teaching for three months and Mr Andrews was expelled as a Marxist troublemaker (something which pleased me no end).

Strangely Mr Andrews bore no grudges, saying, 'What can you expect from a colonial power' and at a farewell party gave a speech in which he prophesied that Emoti would eventually become leader of the country. He expected his pupil to be pleased but the affair had shaken Emo more than anyone realised. It took him a long time to get over the fact that an article could cause so much turmoil and that words alone had caused him to lose his mentor. It had never occurred to him that the written word could be so potent. What further troubled him was that others of his generation tried to prod him into becoming some sort of spokesman for their criticisms of whites and those blacks who would lead us after independence. Emo retreated from any such responsibility. Now that his mentor had gone his own thoughts were confused. He hated his blackness, he loved it. He hated whites, he loved them. During his time away from teaching he withdrew into himself and sometimes when I returned home from school I found him lying on the floor staring up at the angel as if seeking protection from the demons he had unleashed. Not wanting to become involved in anything like that again he spent most of his time with me. It was a time when he was at his most tender and loving. The books on politics were left unopened and to pass the time alone while I was at school he re-read his precious *Phantom* comics, seeking refuge in a jungle world that was much simpler than the world in which he now found himself.

Other countries achieved their independence because they fought for it but ours arrived almost without us having to ask for it. Emo and I went down to the football ground, named Independence Hill for the occasion, and saw the king and queen of England drive around the football ground in a jeep, waving at us. They were exactly like those cut-outs of royals Mister Bacon's daughter had pasted on her bedroom walls. We waved back until our arms were sore and then the loudspeaker told us to look up into the sky. A plane flew over and a man fell out of it. The whole crowd gasped, thinking he was going to fall to his death, but about half way down what looked like a huge mushroom sprouted from his back and he began to glide towards earth like a bird, his left foot trailing red smoke. The tension had been so great that when he touched the ground we all laughed, pretending we knew all along what was going to happen. The man walked to the queen of England and gave her a package, which she in turn gave to our President. The Australian flag was taken down from the flag pole and our flag was unwrapped from the package and raised up to replace that of our former master. As it was being raised a roar went up from the crowd. Even tribesmen with arse grass and pig tusks through their noses shouted with excitement because although they didn't fully understand independence they knew the significance of the flag; our country had become ours. Emo and I wept. I don't think either of us had ever been so proud to be who we were. I for one had never thought I would be so moved at seeing the end of our colonial era.

After the royalty and important people had gone to Government House we celebrated at the football ground, dancing, singing and feasting. Emo danced with an abandon I had never seen before. People were excited to the point of frenzy. When fire crackers exploded over our heads Emo joined in the sounds with animal calls and forest noises. This gift for animal mimicry was totally unexpected, as if he had briefly lapsed back into his tribal ways. He smiled at me through the dancers as if to say *you didn't expect me to be able to do that, did you?* I replied with the calls of the bird of paradise. Everyone was drunk with beer and exhilaration.

Much later that night we headed off into the city with some friends, crying out, 'The city is ours!' In the Chinese district youths were smashing shop windows. Everyone hated the Jews of the Pacific so we joined in, picking up stones and rocks from the road and breaking all the windows in the street. The Chinese had fled to the hills for the night, knowing full well what was coming, and so we had the shops to ourselves. Some policemen arrived. They were drunk on independence too and immediately joined in our attack on the stores that had overcharged us. We broke into the shops, rampaging through them, breaking, smashing and looting. Bottles were thrown against the walls, flour, rice and biscuits were thrown at each other until we were all coated in food. Emo and I gorged ourselves on a tin of cabin crackers and a jar of strawberry jam. A policeman ate a whole can of gherkins and fainted at our feet. Others stole as much food as they could carry and headed off into the night to picnic. Emo and I left the shops and headed towards the fields, laughing and singing, covered in flour like parodies of white men. In the long grass we rubbed our treacley cheeks until they bled and then we made love. Afterwards, while we were resting in each other's arms, we heard noises nearby. Peeking up over the long grass we saw hundreds of celebrators heading back to the football ground. We joined in, singing and dancing the night away until, exhausted, we slept where we fell.

In the morning the whites drove past, their faces expressing condescension at our drunken state and also fear. It was the first time I had ever seen whites openly showing their fear of blacks. It made me feel exhilarated, and it also made me realise how used I was to seeing whites as natural leaders. Now we were in control, we had the power and they were afraid of what we would do with that power. When Emo awoke he was astonished to see me making rude faces at the passing cars but pretty soon he joined in and as we walked home, hungover and excited, past the wailing Chinese inspecting their damaged shops, we continued to pull faces at those ghostly whites passing into history.

How extraordinarily naive and silly we were! We did not become independent from whites because without them our country would have ground to a halt. Most of the politicians may have been black but the actual running of the country needed the expertise of whites and those that remained lived in splendid barbed wire isolation owing allegiance to no one but their bank account. They openly sniggered when one of the President's first decrees was that golf would be our national recreation. When people heard this they flocked to our three golf courses and gawked at the white men, plus the occasional black, playing it, wondering how such a game had become a national recreation when most of us couldn't afford to play. Some of my students, realising they could never aspire to actually playing such an expensive game, decided they would become caddies. For months they carried

86

sticks back and forth across the steaming, muddy playground, pretending they were on a golf course caddying for the President.

Independence became a refuge for all sorts of sickness. Sensing that something monumental had happened to their country but not quite knowing what, everyone began to believe that their dreams would finally be fullfilled. Just as their fathers had believed that praying to the king of England or the American president would result in Western goods falling out of the sky, so these villagers from the backblocks believed that if they came to the capital all they had to do was ask and the fridges, TVs and radios would be theirs. Everything the white man had denied them would now rightfully belong to them. And so they flocked to the city, these men in arse grass and tee shirts and women in pandanus leaf skirts or cheap general store frocks, to ask that their dreams become real.

In a year the population of the capital doubled and the city began to overflow with thousands of the lost and disillusioned. They wandered the streets, aimless and rootless, hoping against hope, that the toasters and air-conditioners imprisoned behind the iron gratings on all store windows would escape into their arms or that they would accidentally stumble on a biscuit tin of money. To ease the pain of broken dreams and being unable to return home to the villages for fear of losing face, the men turned to drink and violence and the women sold themselves. The whites hid behind their barbed wire fortresses and crowed, 'There, isn't that proof enough that you were not ready for independence.' Sometimes I had to agree with them. One evening I came home from school to find that our house had been robbed. The burglars had stolen everything they could carry, pissed and shat on my books and placed Emo's angel on our portable gas stove until it melted into a foul lump of grey plastic. In the Parliament a minister got so drunk that he pissed on the foyer carpets, another used his flash ministerial car to attract women and rape them with the help of his chauffeur. Gangs formed and tribal warfare broke out in the streets. Police were corrupt and politicians represented their tribe rather than the country.

Our rapid disintegration appalled Emo. Independence Day had so filled him with enthusiasm that he, too, found his dreams shattered. Angry at our abrupt decay he wrote articles for newspapers and magazines, not caring if he were dismissed from his teaching position. The government was so weak that although it tried to censor the articles, it did not dismiss him or stop him from speaking out at meetings. These articles and speeches about the government's weakness and corruption made him well known. Our house became a centre for all those who wanted to get rid of the government. We were not radicals in the accepted sense (though you would like people to think you were in those days) but people brought together out of a sense of shame and frustration at what was happening to our country. It was an exciting, though precarious time.

Emo grew even more well known when an Australian journalist interviewed him for a Sydney newspaper and wrote of him as the 'young firebrand the government rightly fears'. He pretended that the article meant nothing to him but to be recognised by the Western press meant much to him. He kept the article in an exercise book and occasionally I caught him re-reading it or just staring at it and touching it in the distant, lingering way he gazed at me after we had made love. When he was out of the house I would look at the article and stare at the fuzzy picture of my husband and think to myself *that is my Emo, he is famous*. His confidence grew as did his ability to attract people or convert them to his ideas. Some of the people who came to our house to talk to him looked at him with nothing short of adoration. The attention began to change him. He became sharper with people whom he didn't agree with and openly derided those who still clung to tribal beliefs. 'This is what tribal life does to you,' he would say, holding up his two deformed fingers. It was difficult to refrain from smiling when he did this because they were the very fingers he liked to slide up my vagina when we made love. After withdrawing them he licked and sucked the misshapen remnants of his tribal life as if they were a delicious lolly. Those days, of course, a wife's secret knowledge of her husband was no threat to you.

One evening a newcomer addressed a meeting in our house and spoke of killing all whites. The room went quiet. Even though some had thought of this no one had ever voiced it. All eyes turned to Emo and I realised at that moment just how crucial he was to these people. Like some of the others he seemed stunned by the outburst, then he quickly regained his composure, 'We don't want another Haiti revolution on our hands, do we?' No one in the room knew what he meant and this gave him the breathing space to collect his thoughts. Then he went on, 'We don't want to kill the whites. We'll send back those who just want to make a quick buck but we want those who will help us to stay. We need Western countries to teach us about technology and the modern world because if we don't learn our country will have a bloodbath on its hands.'

The newcomer persisted. 'But do you want to get rid of certain whites?'

'Of course.'

The applause was deafening, it thundered over the rain that was pouring down on our corrugated roof. It wasn't so much his answer that excited people but his certainty. The people in that room knew they had found a leader and he knew he had made a breakthrough. Too excited to sleep he spent the night walking in the garden talking to himself. What were you talking about? You can tell me now. Perhaps you were trying to calm yourself. Perhaps your brain was so full of brilliant visions of your future that everything seemed too wonderfully possible. I watched you from the window as you daydreamt under the stars. An owl swept down on a fleeing mouse near your feet. In a sudden movement you reached out and caught the owl and looked into its huge yellow eyes as if saying to it *nothing is beyond me tonight*. Next morning, however, the euphoria vanished. The newspaper headline was 'CALL TO GET RID OF WHITES: FUTURE BLOODBATH'.

The newcomer had been an agent provocateur. The government had formed an alliance with important whites and they were becoming increasingly afraid that Emoti was unsettling potential investors who thought he was a Marxist revolutionary and that the government was going to get caught up in a costly civil war. The newspaper article gave the government the excuse it needed. Emo was suspended from teaching, he was forbidden to address any meetings and it was made illegal for more than three people to be in our house. We were under virtual house arrest. The only money coming in was through my teaching. The government's actions astonished Emo. It is curious but he never thought anything would happen to him, not because he believed he was invincible but because he could not match the punishment he received with what he was talking about. In those days he found it hard to understand the consequences of his words or deeds. The punishment profoundly depressed him. Above all he hated the new isolation; he had begun to enjoy all those people around him and the importance of his role. What of the stories of him secretly visiting his friends late at night and setting up clandestine anti-government groups? Another fib. The owl had the night to himself. As before when under pressure he retreated into a silent world of his own to which I was not allowed entry.

Friends began to pass rumours on to me that the government was going to frame him by planting evidence of an armed uprising in our house. It was also said that on a raid to find such evidence the police would kill Emo. I pleaded with Emo that we go into exile as some had suggested. He did not listen to me. At night I would catch him staring at me as if he had been doing so for quite some time. I pretended not to notice these incidents but a great fear grew inside me. I began to suspect that I was a burden to him, that my pleading for us to leave was repulsive to him. I thought he viewed me as a coward who did not realise the issues at stake and did not understand the importance of his staying and confronting the government. It was simple to me: I loved him and didn't want to lose him. He was the most important thing in the world to me. The rumours that he might be killed were not fiction to me but true. The signs were everywhere. Bats began to fly over our house. Poinsettias at the front of our house burst into bloom out of season as if the scarlet flowers were predicting a bloody event. To torment us government agents would wander on to our garden, pretending to be hicks from the backblocks and shit on my taro and cassava. If an agent saw us looking at him through our window he would take out his gun and rub it hard as if masturbating it. To try and protect us I sprinkled my menstrual blood on the front door step so that if the police ever stood there they would get sick. I also stuck yellow oxalis flowers on the front and back doors to protect the house from evil. Emo called me silly but did not remove them.

One night I awoke and found that his side of the bed was empty. I got up and went to the doorway that led into our other room. Emo was in the middle of the room, on his knees, murmuring something quietly but urgently. In front of him was a small wooden statue of an angel about two feet high. He must have secretly bought it to replace the destroyed angel. I had never seen him so distraught or at such a loss. He felt my presence and turned to me. 'Get out!' he hissed. I didn't move and he turned back to the angel. After a time he said, as he stared at it, 'I am scared. You're right, we should go into exile.' I rushed to him and hugged him.

In the relief of having made the decision we made love. As he lay on top of me the angel flew up above me, its serious expression having changed into a smile. I knew then that the angel had talked Emo into it. When I climaxed the angel flew across the room in delirious loops of happiness. 'Palu,' I remembered Mister Bacon once saying to me, 'you have plugged into some electric current of life and are always short circuiting into happiness.'

After making love Emo lay on top of me and whispered in my ear, 'I love you'. Oh, Angel, I am up with you in seventh, eighth, tenth heaven. It was one of the few occasions he ever said it to me, not because he didn't feel it but because his language, like mine, didn't have the words, the nearest being, 'I lust after you'. The only way we could express this deepest of all feelings was to use a foreign language. I can still feel his maleness enveloping me at that moment and I can still hear your whisper. Yet it is not loud enough to block out the noises around me. I follow the direction of the gecko's gaze. He is staring into the corridor where the guards are whispering. Some old guard has found wild taro and the guards are rubbing it on their genitals. Tonight they will become bats and slaughter more prisoners. Already I can hear the whistling of bloodlust. Angel gecko, beat your wings, carry me to Australia like the jet plane. Leave the whistling behind.

AUSTRALIA! AUSTRALIA! It sounded like the mysterious incantation of a sorcerer. The little I knew about it I had learnt from Mister Bacon, who had long been exiled from it, and from the poems and stories of Henry Lawson. I expected a landscape like dried up tissue paper and rugged farmers harvesting wheat and so I was unprepared for Sydney.

We were met by Mr Andrews and his new wife, Louise, an attractive woman with large smiling teeth who kissed me in a cloud of perfume and long hair. Mr Andrews, whom we were told to call Ted, fussed about us and said things which I could not take in because my senses were under assault by whiteness; white walls, white ceilings and piercing fluorescent lights. Emo and I were like two black fishes being tossed about in a churning white ocean. Shivering in the cold air-conditioning, we tried not to gawk. We tried to pretend we were unfazed by it all but it was impossible for us to hide our amazement at this new world. A few hours before you had been a threat to the government, but in this foreign light you were just an anonymous black man with bedazzled eyes, wearing shorts and sandshoes. And there is your spooked wife, a midget amidst giants, standing so close to you that she is about to become part of you. She wears a simple cotton dress, which she once thought was *so* stylish, and the orchids have wilted in her frizzy hair.

It was twilight when we left the airport. The Andrews chatted to us as they drove to their inner city home but we could not listen. There were too many extraordinary things to see. Where do we look? What do we look at? Buildings touched the sky, cars, so numerous they were like a plague of locusts, roared around us and neon lights burst into our eyes. Never, not even in my wildest dreams, had I imagined lights like sunbursts, noises like the inferno of a bat's cave or the sheer number of people who swirled through the immense, twinkling streets.

Drowning under a sea of impressions we could not sleep that first night. We felt as if we had arrived on another planet. Unable to believe I could live in this hectic, overbearing world, and feeling guilty that I had pleaded with Emo to go into an Australian exile, I cried to myself, while Emo, as awestruck as I, took refuge in a benumbed silence. We sat up in bed all night, unable to close our dazzled eyes.

In the morning the Andrews went to work, leaving us alone in the house. After they had gone Emo, exhausted, drifted off to sleep. I was too excited to sleep and I set out to explore the house. The lounge room was as opulent as a magazine illustration; paintings on every wall and a carpet as soft and spongy as sago pulp. I was heading into the next room when I spotted the television in the corner. I had never seen a real television and I spent some minutes fiddling with the knobs before I was able to turn it on. All the things I had heard about television did not prepare me for its impact; it was like a box filled with astonishing, delirious dreams. When I put my hand on the screen it crackled as if I were touching its spirit. Mr Gecko, you cannot imagine my naive wonderment as I flicked from channel to channel trying to absorb a world so large and marvellous that my brain could take in very little of it. Hearing the noises of the television Emo got up and joined me. Entranced, we sat before the pulsating screen until hunger forced us to find food.

The kitchen had an enormous fridge, which was nothing like the kerosene ones I had been used to. Its bright interior light shone on the full shelves of food, as if creating a piece of theatre. Everything in Australia was white and brilliant. Wanting to be astonished further I turned on every switch I could find in the house. By the time I had finished every light was on, the radio was singing, the mix-master and juice extractor whirred around, a carving knife flopped on the sink like a just landed fish, electric blankets roasted the beds, fans and air-conditioners hummed and stove plates glowed red hot. Excited by it all, I ran, dancing, through the rooms; it was as if the cheering, screaming noises were electrical spirits that had joyously possessed the house. At the sink I accidentally turned on another switch and a growling, spinning noise erupted from deep inside it. I was about to put my hand down the plughole to find out what it was, when a woman screamed out.

'Palu. No!'

It was Louise, she had arrived home. She looked around at the whirring, jubilant world I had created.

'Palu, what have you done?'

'I was trying them out.'

Louise said nothing but I knew she was annoyed. Before going around the house and switching off everything I had turned on, she took a carrot out of the fridge and put it down the squealing plughole. It devoured the carrot like some starving monster. I shivered at the thought of what I had almost done to my hand.

Ted laughed when told of what I had done. He saw me as a child and mockingly chided me with 'curiosity killed the cat'. Knowing how inquisitive I was he asked me if there was anything I especially wanted to see in Australia. When I told him that I wanted to see the countryside he organised a picnic, just outside of Sydney, for the four of us.

I was profoundly disappointed. This wasn't the dusty outback. It was a ferny, almost English green valley. Ted saw my disappointment and asked me what I had expected. I told him of the Australia I knew from the writings of Henry Lawson; the world of Joe Wilson and his mates. I wanted to see where the drover's wife had heroically fought off the snake that came to kill her children. I wanted to see the waterhole where Tommy, the dog, almost blew up his master and, especially, I wanted to see the tree where Joe had seen his vision of a woman who would come to save his sick son.

'That's the outback of Australia, Palu,' Ted explained. 'It's a long way away and quite foreign to most Australians.'

He was curious to know how I had come to know so much about Australia's great writer. I could not tell him about Mister Bacon because Emo bridled at the very mention of his name and so I went quiet, thinking of those wonderful stories that had so gripped my imagination when I was younger, while the other three talked politics.

It is extraordinary how quickly one can get used to new things. In a few weeks we took for granted all the gadgets in the Andrews' household, everything except the television which we watched from the time we got up until the time we went to bed. We watched anything; soap operas, cartoons, quiz shows, the news, and old movies. I could not get over the diversity of Western life and its hurry; white people always walked fast as if perpetually late. Naive and oblivious to everything except our own curiosity we did not realise that we were wearing out our welcome until one night at dinner, Ted told us that he had arranged for us to stay at his mother's flat which was only a few streets away. They would give it to us rent free but we had to pay our living costs. Louise had spoken to a friend of hers who ran a cleaning service and had recommended me as a cleaner. I was offended. 'I'm not going to clean house! I am not a servant!'

Emo looked at me despairingly. I could see what was in his eyes *there she is on her high horse again*. I could not go back to being a servant again. It would have been too humiliating. I wanted to teach or just stay at home while Emo taught but the trouble was that our qualifications were not recognised in Australia.

I was sick to the stomach when I showed up at a house on the other side of the city a few days later. The woman who answered the door was surprised to see me. 'But I distinctly asked for a Portuguese or Spanish cleaning lady,' she said, and leaving me standing in the doorway, rang the cleaning agency to protest but to no avail. The woman, Mrs Gibbs, bustled me inside and thrust in my hand a piece of paper with a list of all the jobs I had to do. 'Can you read English?' When I said I could she went on, 'Well that's a relief, most of the women I have can't even read their own languages.' With that she left for work.

I felt as if I had been stranded on a desert island. Depressed and humiliated I sat in a chair for a long time debating with myself whether I should just leave and never return, but as Emo and I needed the money I set about cleaning the house. I knew how to make beds and clean floors but I had no idea how the washing machine or vacuum cleaner worked. By the time Mrs Gibbs returned from work the clothes were covered in soap powder but still unwashed and the vacuum cleaner was in several pieces. I gave a silly smile when she saw the vacuum cleaner but when she demanded to know what had gone wrong I could do nothing but cry. She shook her head and put the pieces back together. 'Jesus, you're bloody lucky there's a shortage of cleaners.' I wanted her to tell me I was fired, instead she showed me how to work the machines and when I returned to our flat that evening, I was on the way to becoming a proper cleaning lady.

I cleaned four homes a week, all belonging to married families, the exception being Mrs Lockwood, a divorcee. Although she worked I sometimes found her still home when I arrived, sitting in front of a dead fire crying. On these occasions I felt the true lowly nature of my position because although I wanted to comfort her, I realised that a black servant had no right to be offering comfort to her white employer. Not knowing what to do I vacuumed around her, pretending I did not notice that she was there. One time I caught her twenty-year-old son with his arm around her, telling her, 'I think it's time you changed your psychiatrist or maybe went on a new diet.'

My favourite employer was Mr Vine. A middle-aged, chubby man who worked out of home, he had gold-capped teeth and when he smiled his mouth shone like the sun. I would do childish things like making silly faces just to see him smile. 'You're a real card, Palu,' he would say and I would behave even more outrageously, singing songs or stuffing my mouth with ping-pong balls. I told him lies about my past because his mouth would open with amazement on hearing he had a cannibal as a cleaner and if I were close enough I could see right down his mouth as if I were peering into a golden cave.

I soon learnt that the major preoccupation of Australians was sex. One morning I came upon a naked woman in the Moores' kitchen. The woman yelped when she saw me and

Mr Moore came hurrying out of the bedroom, naked and hairy like an ape. 'Oh, shit!' he said on seeing me with a wettex in my hand. 'This is the cleaning lady,' he explained to the naked woman, 'I forgot that today is Wednesday.'

'Great,' she said sarcastically. Mr Moore wondered how to explain his adultery to me. In the silence that followed, all that the three of us could hear was the water dripping, drop by drop, onto the floor from my sponge. I was repulsed by all his hair. It grew everywhere, covering his chest and legs and even sprouting from his back. Finally he motioned to the woman. 'This is my cousin, she's staying here for the day. She and my wife don't get on, so it's probably best not to mention this visit to her.' I nodded as if I were a stupid nigger and, whistling a tune to indicate my mindlessness, I started wiping down the sink. The naked couple returned to the bedroom and whispered feverishly for a time until the woman got dressed and angrily left the house.

One Monday when I arrived at Mrs Lockwood's home I was surprised to see her looking radiant. 'Isn't this a nice morning, Palu?' she said happily and hurried off to work. I was busy cleaning the lounge room when I heard a noise from upstairs. My blood went cold. I was afraid it might be the rapist-murderer who was being talked about in the news. I heard another noise and saw a black figure descending the stairs. For an awful moment I thought it was a ghost from my homeland coming to meet me then I realised that this naked man had African features. He didn't see me until he was almost at the bottom stair. Our eyes met and we both stood still, astonished to see another black face in such circumstances. He didn't know what to say. The small black woman staring up at him unnerved him because it reminded him of his position. Just as a black woman was servicing Mrs Lockwood by cleaning the house so he, a black man, had serviced her in bed. We were momentarily bound together by the knowledge of our demeaning roles. There was no need to say anything and after a shower he quickly left, having served his purpose in making Mrs Lockwood momentarily forget her despair. Oh, I tell you, Mr Gecko, I wanted to set fire to that house then and there. That black man reminded me of just how much I hated being a servant again and how homesick I was.

Emo didn't feel the pain of exile as keenly as I. He had a purpose, believing that the exile was a necessary prelude to a triumphal return home. He studied some political subjects at university and Ted arranged for him to do some part-time work for the Teachers' Union, of which Ted was one of the main organisers. The work allowed Emo to travel to other Australian states and meet up with the growing number of exiles. Ted also took him to political meetings and soon Emo became recognised as the leader of the exiles.

Leftwing Australians fawned over Emo, seeing in his blackness the Third World righteousness of his cause. He regained the energy he had lost while under house arrest and grew tremendously persuasive, especially in gaining the support of those of our countrymen who were studying in Australian universities and who had little or no interest in getting rid of the present government. His main opposition was the son of a cabinet minister who was studying agriculture at Melbourne university. Emo knew that if he could win him over then others who were reluctant would join him.

Although intelligent, Tingue was a bit of a playboy and saw Emo as a threat to the privileges he had quickly grown used to. Tingue, also, did not want to betray his father — well, that was his excuse when he replied to Emo's letters. Knowing that the only way he could alter Tingue's attitude was to meet him, Emo decided to go to Melbourne. Although the trip would be expensive he asked me if I wanted to come with him to that southern city. Of course I wanted to go, I wanted to be always with Emo. We went by train and arrived on a wet and freezing Spring day. A cold wind blew through our light clothes and cut into our skin. The people wore coats and gloomy expressions. It reminded me of a city described by Dickens in one of his darkest moods.

In order to impress us, Tingue met us in a new car and took us into the centre of the city where a parade was being held in the rain; floats representing myths and achievements were led by the most beautiful woman in the state. We stood in the cold, our teeth chattering, until even Tingue, who had wanted to impress us with his stoicism, could take no more. That night he took us to an expensive restaurant. Handsome and humorous, Tingue's face was puffy from the good life. He knew little of politics nor did he really care. He seemed more interested in what he wanted to order than any talk about ideologies. Suspicious of Emo he set out to shame us by showing us which of the numerous pieces of cutlery to use. Instead of showing his annoyance Emo seemed humble, even playing up his ignorance of such things. He did not drink the wine, as if he were a tribal villager who had had the fear of alcohol so drummed into him by missionaries that he was too scared to even take a drop. Tingue was amused by Emo's reluctance and teased him about being a puritan. I grew merry as did Tingue while Emo, a few years older than Tingue, began to adopt the attitude of an older brother towards his younger, wayward brother, telling Tingue that he hoped he would not be too sidetracked by Western living and would get his degree because the country urgently needed agricultural scientists. Tingue grew annoyed at Emo's seeming moral superiority and then suddenly expressed his greatest fear.

101

'You want to kill my father.'

'I don't. I just want to get rid of corrupt politicians. Don't you want our country to be uncorrupt?'

'Yes, I do,' said Tingue, unaware of just how incongruous his statement was, given that his wealth was created by his father's milking of the treasury of which he was minister.

'That's all we want. Just to get rid of the corrupt and inefficient. You can't argue with that can you?'

'No,' Tingue said quietly, staring at the messy remains of a fish skeleton on his plate. He turned to me.

'Do you think my father is corrupt, Palu?' His question startled me, I was unprepared for such a serious question. I looked to Emo who smiled encouragement, not in the least surprised that Tingue should ask me such a thing. I understood immediately why Emo had asked me if I wanted to accompany him on this trip. Tingue and I were Highlanders and so Tingue would trust me more than he trusted Emo. I had an obligation to answer a fellow Highlander as truthfully as possible.

'I think he's a bit corrupt.'

Emo grimaced but Tingue smiled broadly. 'I think he is, too,' he said, staring at his glass of wine as if mesmerised by it. 'But not as corrupt as others?'

'No.'

He looked across at Emo in the flickering candlelight. 'Fifteen years ago he was a tribesman wearing arse grass and mud masks,' he said, explaining, as succinctly as possible, how a man like that would have been easily corrupted by the temptations of government.

'I understand.'

'I will not betray him, Emoti.'

Emo nodded. A distant door opened and a cold burst of wind hit us, momentarily chilling us. It was a reminder to

102

Tingue of what Emo wanted to do to our country. It froze his bones, but he knew it had to happen. His voice grew soft and the whispering roundness of his face seemed to vanish and be replaced by that of a youth. 'I wanted to get away from the tropics, as far as possible,' he said, smiling as the rain flecked the window beside us. I saw in him a great confusion, a bewilderment even more profound than that which a villager experiences on seeing Port Andrews for the first time. Tingue wanted to distance himself as much as possible — from his country, from his colour. Haunted by self-hatred and hatred for his backward country, he took refuge in trivialities and sex. He saw in Emo a man who had all the energy and courage he wanted but lacked. Emo was temporarily in exile, Tingue was running away and would never return home.

'If you promise to give my father another chance, I'll agree not to speak against your group.'

'I can't. I can only promise that he will not be harmed or jailed.'

Tingue nodded, respecting Emo's honesty. Emo and he shook hands. Tipsy, I giggled at the Western mannerism. They thought I was merely showing my pleasure at their agreement. Tingue toasted me, 'To Palu—no better Highlander.'

Now that the agreement had been reached, Emo relented and drank some wine. I stared at him openly in the candlelight, admiring him immensely. He had done it — he had won over Tingue! Mr Gecko, he could charm or talk the birds from the trees.

Poor Tingue, I often wonder what happened to him. It was rumoured that he went to Europe soon afterwards and died there of a drug overdose. There were a few like him; Emo called them 'the lost'. Young men who became ashamed of their country, once they were in Australia or Europe, and who would never return to their homeland but would wander endlessly; black men in cold and indifferent climates. Some, of course, openly embraced what Emo talked about, seeing his idealism and verve as something they knew was needed to help our country as it grew more inept. Emo joked, stroked, argued with and finally won over all those he wanted to so that he developed, in a remarkably short time, an Australian network of exiles opposed to the government back home.

When he had had a successful meeting he would glow like a black sun. When he made love to me, I swear to you, Mr Gecko, my skin burnt with his energy. Oh, my black prince, you made my exile bearable then. Our bed was an oasis from the blizzard outside.

Louise tried to take an interest in me but as far as she was concerned I was merely the wife of a political exile. Like Ted her life was politics, and she spent much of her time, when not lecturing at university, in organising marches for various causes, especially feminist ones. Concerned that I seemed depressed when Emo went interstate with Ted, she organised a lunch for me with several of her friends. It was the worst thing she could have done; they all looked so calm and attractive; I felt like a black beetle amidst newly opened flowers. After tiring of asking me questions about my country and the oppression of women there, they began to talk openly about orgasms and sanitary napkins. I had discovered in my cleaning job just how brazen Australian women were. Nothing was sacred or held mystery for them. Women kissed men full on the lips in broad daylight and talked openly to men about their menstruation. Didn't these women understand that by telling men all their secrets they lost their power and their magic? When I told them I slept apart from Emo each month they laughed and looked at me as if I were crazy but I knew the power of good and bad blood. I had seen a market garden in the Highlands destroyed because some stupid girl had walked through it when she had her period.

When Louise was making tea in the kitchen I overheard her telling one of the other women, 'Palu's lost in Australia. She's become a bit of a burden to her husband'. I tried to hear more but one of the women kept yapping at me about her grandfather who had been part of the colonial admin- istration of my country (she wanted to appear critical of that part of Australian history, but like the English and their nostalgic affection for the British Raj, her eyes expressed a longing for that era). When Louise returned to the living room with the tea I wanted to scratch her eyes out, instead I pleaded a headache and left.

On the way home I saw a bus and its destination read: Rozelle. *Rozelle*! That's where a good many married folk dwell. I hurried over to the bus and got on it. When I arrived in Rozelle I went looking for the brick and red tiled houses Henry Lawson had talked about. I found some in a narrow street and wondered if Lawson, too, had stood on the very spot where I was, thinking about the people who lived in those houses. I began to feel happy again because it brought back memories of Mister Bacon and I realised just how far I had come in such a short time. Rozelle had always seemed like a mysterious isle to me, full of enchantment and happiness and although it was in reality a drab, working class suburb, the very idea that Lawson could create such an exulted cry of happiness out of it made it seem magical.

I half expected to hear cries of 'Ripperty Kye A-hoo' coming from inside the houses. I asked an old lady where the sea was and she pointed me in its direction. I went down a hill and came upon a pier where several shoes sat waiting on its edge. I puzzled over why the shoes were empty and placed where they were. Perhaps they belonged to people who had been kidnapped by spacemen, something a TV news reporter had talked about when explaining the disappearance of several Japanese women in Paris. I examined the shoes looking for the tell-tale evidence of burns caused by the beams of light which transported victims into the spacecraft. A voice yelled out, 'What are you doing with our shoes?' I looked up into the sky and out of the corner of my eye I saw a man approaching me across the water. As he came closer I saw he was in a canoe. I held up a pair of shoes. 'Do these belong to you?'

'Me and those others there,' he said, motioning across the twilight waters to a much larger canoe with four people in it.

I stood about and watched the rowers return, dragging their boats out of the water and washing them down before putting them in the boatshed. The men reminded me of when I was young watching fishermen row down the river near my village. The rowers found my interest in their rowboats amusing and they said I was welcome to come down to the rowing club anytime I wished. I took them at their word and would often go down to watch them practise when Emo was away and I was feeling lonely. Just before dusk the sun would shine onto the nearby city and the glass skyscrapers would be transformed into golden palaces and the water would shine like liquid coal. The men got to know me and I became like their mascot. After practice they often bought me a beer in the clubhouse and I would regale them with stories about life in the jungle and cannibal feasts. If Emo were away on race days I went along to cheer my team to victory and if they won I cried out, 'Ripperty Kye A-hoo — Rozelle is where the rowers dwell.' It is a lie to say I fucked these men. I have heard the guards say that I am a witch who fucked rowing teams when she was in Australia. Only men would believe such nonsense. Only a man would invent such a lie. When I told you of how much time I spent watching the rowers you slapped me and called me a whore. I tried to explain that I was innocent and you shouted, 'No woman can behave like that and still be innocent. Those rowers want you because you behave like you want to be wanted.' Your jealousy proved to me that you still loved me and so I stopped going to the rowing club but a figment of your imagination grew into the truth.

Some *more* lies about the time in Australia: I did not say we should live there permanently and that you should give up the idea of returning here. You know very well that I hated being in exile and being a servant in white households. I am yelling this out *it is a lie*! You may be able to fool the Night People but not others. Whatever you decided in Australia I went along with. I was a pale moon revolving around your black sun.

Also: I did not kill suburban cats in order to use their blood for witchcraft.

I did not sneak after you at university 'spying on you like a bad dream'. I turned up once, after cleaning, to see what university was like. Your bad dream will come upon you in another way.

I did not spend all my money on clothes.

I did not steal from my employers. Once or twice I may have tried on some perfume. There were occasions when I tried on Mrs Gibbs' dresses and although she was the smallest woman I worked for her clothes were still too big for me. Her dresses were exquisite but they made me look like a child pretending to be a woman. She had a beautiful dresser

107

and mirror with every type of make-up. I stared at the black face in her mirror staring back at me and cursed my blackness because all the make-up before me was useless on my skin. My face seemed coarse and insensitive as if it had been corrupted by the night. You, Mr Gecko, who have only seen shades of blackness, have no idea of what it is like to live among only white faces and Australians are *so* white.

Last night guards burst into my cell as I slept and ransacked it looking for something. They would not tell me what. They had just come from killing some prisoners and they were talking and yelling excitedly, in that potent mixture of fear and bloodlust. They told me how they had sliced off their victims' crowns, baring the brains, and watched the dying perform contorted leaps like headless chickens. They wanted to scare me shitless. They yelled at me and tore apart my bed and table. I wasn't too scared because I knew that, for the moment, I was going to live. Although they hovered around me, yelling at me, they did not touch me. I still had the protective aura of being the President's wife. The thing is, were they searching for something specific or had the governor told them to come and harass me, realising that in their hysterical condition they would not be so in awe of me? After they had gone I sat on the concrete floor and thought of you. Where are you now? Are you sleepless and also sitting on your marble tiled floor thinking of me, wondering if you should release me? I will match you emotion for emotion and I will beat you. And what about you, Mr Gecko, I suspect you are a coward. It took you a long time to emerge from your crack in the wall and, as if apologising for your cowardice, you serenaded me with soft barking. It was while the gecko was singing to me that my guard came in, as if wanting to see the damage first hand. I accused him of sending the others in here to search for my paper and pen. He denied it. I did not know whether to believe him or not. The early morning wind blew through the window into my cell, bringing with it the smell of slaughter. The gecko hurried back into his hiding place, wheezing in fear. My guard smelt it too and in the piccaninny light I saw how young he was, perhaps only nineteen. I asked him his name.

'Nambweapa'w.'

I laughed. Night People's names are as long as a rock python. He looked offended. I wanted to say that I wasn't laughing at him but I was not going to apologise. Just grab me, I wanted to say, hug me to your chest because I am afraid. I may look calm and self-possessed but I am shivering inside. The smell of last night's victims is all around me while you stand before me thinking *this witch is causing me all sorts of trouble*. I asked him for a bed. After returning with one he silently put it together for me. I thought to myself *is he doing this for me or has the governor said 'scare the shit out of her and then a couple of hours later give her another bed and she'll be pathetically grateful for it'?* After the bed was completed (once, in another time, Nambweapa'w, you would have been a wonderful tribal crafts-man making boats or sculptures for spirit houses) he stepped back and stared at me; we both looked haggard in the morning light. What did he see when he looked at me? A President's wife? A woman he lusted after? A witch? Maybe all three: wife, woman, witch. Maybe that is it. I am a bundle of confusions for him and that is why he hates me. If I were not the President's wife he would have killed me to relieve himself of the terrible tension of confusion.

The longer we stayed in Australia the more at ease I grew

with Western things but one morning, as I was cleaning Mrs Gibbs' bedroom, I came upon a strange object on the floor. It was like the pale skin of a baby snake; it was exactly like the mysterious white man's object my father and I had puzzled over in the spirit house. When Mrs Gibbs came home I showed it to her, wanting to uncover the mystery of these peculiar objects. She was amazed at what I held in my hand and asked me where I had found it.

'Next to your bed.'

'But surely you know what it is, Palu?'

I shook my head and told her of the white man's amulets my father and I had seen. She started to laugh but stopped when she saw my genuine bewilderment. 'You really don't know what it is?'

I held it up to the light and for the life of me I had no idea.

'It's a rubber,' she said, grimacing as I touched and fondled the object.

'To rub out things?'

'It's a term... it's a covering for a man's penis.'

I laughed, Mrs Gibbs was kidding me. 'I know that white people put clothes on everything but no one would put clothes on a manhood.'

'Men do it, Palu, so women won't get pregnant. It stops the sperm from getting into the womb.'

All of this was totally alien to me. It made no sense to have sex if a woman didn't want to get pregnant. I had always wanted a child with Emo and could not understand why Mrs Gibbs, who only had a daughter and was very wealthy, did not want more children. I had solved the mystery of the patrol officer's object but found my discoveries concerning some of the attitudes of Australians really quite unpleasant.

110

Emo, on the other hand, had taken quickly to Australian ways, drinking at the pub with his uni mates, going to endless meetings and even betting on horse races. By immersing himself in this culture he was obliterating the past of which he was ashamed. Once, when we were invited to a display of artefacts from the Highlands at a local shopping centre, he refused to go because to be seen amid primitive objects would make him seem primitive too. I wanted to go because I was homesick and wished to be among my own kind and my own culture. Every time Emo went away I felt dead. My one great wish, to have a child, was left unfulfilled. What made this desire for a child even worse was having to clean up my employers' bedrooms and come upon their contraceptives (pills, condoms and strange rubber contraptions), all used to stop conception. It was as if they were left out on display to mock me. I knew Mrs Moore was having an affair when I discovered a used shiny black condom in her bed while her husband was away and one morning I arrived to find her in bed with a strange man. She paraded around in the kitchen getting him a coffee as I cleaned, saying to me, 'What's good for the goose is good for the gander.' She asked me if I had affairs.

'No, I don't, Mrs Moore. I am faithful to my husband because I love him.'

She looked at me stonily as if I were criticising her and was about to say something when the front door opened and her husband, back a few days early, came in. Colour drained from her face. Her lover was still upstairs in bed. She tried to express joy at her husband's early arrival but all that came out was an anguished squawk. A part of me wanted her to get caught but I found myself as startled and nervous as she was. Her husband noticed her pained expression.

111

'Are you all right, sweetie?'

'Just a bit of a headache, darling.'

She asked me to get her an aspirin. I returned with one and a glass of water. My hand trembled as I put the pill in her hand. She gulped down the water and nearly choked. Her husband hit her on the back until she recovered her breath. Trying to stop him from going upstairs she suddenly pretended great interest in my husband when I said he had nearly choked on a glass of water once. 'What does he do, Palu?'

'He's a revolutionary, Mrs Moore.'

'Oh,' she gasped, 'I thought you said he was a gardener.'

'I think you're getting mixed up with someone else.'

'Is he planning to overthrow the Australian government?'

'My country's government.'

'Oh,' she said, relieved.

Bored by our chatter Mr Moore started up the stairs.

'Don't go up there,' she cried out. He looked back, puzzled. 'Palu hasn't cleaned up there yet.'

'That's all right, I just want to put my bag...'

'Palu will do it! Palu, take Mr Moore's bag upstairs and clean the bedroom. This instant.'

I wanted to rebel and take no more part in this farce but, of course, I obeyed meekly. When I walked into the bedroom I was surprised to see Mrs Moore's lover still there. I thought he would have made some attempt to hide or even flee out the window but he stood, half dressed, at the foot of the bed paralysed with panic. He looked at me as if he half expected me to save him from his predicament. I heard Mrs Moore's cry of alarm and knew her husband was heading up the stairs.

'Palu, I want you to...' he started to say as he entered the room but his words died when he saw a strange man

112

standing before him wearing only a singlet and shorts. The two men stared at one another, incredulous at finding themselves in such a situation. I wanted Mr Moore to throw himself on his wife's boyfriend and beat him, but he seemed just as embarrassed as the lover.

'I think you should go, don't you?' he said softly. The lover nodded, quickly dressed and left. I felt ashamed at Mr Moore's timidity. Didn't he realise that he had been cuckolded? Where was his sense of honour? Mr Gecko, what cowards white men are! They have no sense of self-respect or honour. Such fools!

The next day I found a note under my door from Mrs Moore telling me she was hiring a new cleaner, and although she liked me she had decided it was time for a change. There was no way she was going to have me in her house again. You see, I knew too much for a cleaner, especially a black cleaner whose morals were superior to her own. The stories, Mr Gecko, the stories I could tell about the sexual life of whites. All the anthropologists that study our tribes should go back to their place of birth and study the weird ways of their own people.

One day when I was shopping, a warm, moist sensation enveloped me like a mist. I did not know what to make of this feeling. Walking home I paused in a small park feeling nauseous because of the car and bus fumes and, as I sat on the bench, I began to feel as light as a balloon. I felt myself rising from the bench and as I did the nearby palm tree (which I loved because it reminded me of home) slowly arched backwards and then bent forwards, bowing towards me in the dusk. A wind of excitement blew through me. I recognised the signs. *I was pregnant.* I flew home, almost tripping over a drunken derelict lying on the footpath. You want to know excitement, Mr Gecko, an excitement that even your most shrill cries of joy cannot compete with? See, look, see the black speck hurtling through the streets of Rozelle and Glebe. It is not a piece of carbon paper being blown by the wind, no, it is a deliriously happy woman. Finally, after five years of trying, I was pregnant. Emo could not believe it either. We kissed and rubbed cheeks until we were sore. Like me he had thought that one of us must be infertile. We told the Andrews. They said they were happy for us but we could tell they did not understand how important it was to us.

During the early days of my pregnancy I found a shop that sold large tins of cabin crackers and I sat in bed late into the mornings on the days I didn't have to work devouring cabin crackers and drinking bottle after bottle of soft drinks until Emo began to worry that the baby inside me might be floating in a sea of lemonade. I also drank all the semen Emo could give me. The more I swallowed the greater chance that the child would be chubby and healthy when born. I was insatiable for your penis, remember? If you were limp I would rub you until you were erect again and drain you until you were exhausted and you would joke *it'd better be a boy after all this*. But we always knew he would be a boy, he moved in my belly like a boy.

Before I became pregnant Emo had been spending a lot of time away from home. I had begun to fear I was losing him. When he returned he would quickly grow irritable with me. Where once he had listened to my comments on the drafts of his speeches, he now became angry if I merely hinted at a piece of bad grammar or poorly expressed thought. Once he had asked me to correct his accent but now he began to grow annoyed at me if I did. After the anger would come the silence. *Talk to me, Emo. I know this exile is difficult for the both of us, but just talk to me. I am silently*

*pleading with you, do not sit in front of 'Star Trek', talk
to me!* Without a word he would take some of my hard-
earned money and disappear into the city to return some
hours later with an angel. Another angel? Your black eyes
are smiling, dear gecko, but at the time it was deadly serious.
He discovered Sydney's Catholic shops and whenever he had
money he bought another angel. You should have seen the
second bedroom, it was quite impossible to move around
in it. Angels from an inch high to three foot high. Angels
lit from the inside, others made of wood, some made of
plastic that was so cheap they turned from white to pale
grey in a matter of weeks. Whenever a shop assistant saw
Emo enter he would cross himself for God having favoured
him so. Emo kept his fears from me but the angels expressed
them. I had gotten used to his rhetoric about overthrowing
the corrupt government or returning to fight the army and
I sometimes forgot that he meant what he was saying (a
wife grows used to her husband's extreme words). But all
I needed to convince me was the arrival of another angel.
The more uneasy or afraid he was, the more he sought the
comfort of angels. Sometimes, before he addressed a group
of university academics or a conference on Third World
countries, he would go into the angel room and speak to
his angels as they flew around him offering him their support
and comfort. Unable to tell me about his inner fears he
told these vacant-eyed immortals. The angels were our secret
and whenever anyone else was in the flat the angel door
was locked. Even the Andrews knew nothing about his collection. Why is there no mention of this room in your official
biography? To this day there is a palace door to which only
you hold the key.

But now, as I grew plumper and more pregnant, so did
his love for me. Like the days when we were at teachers'

college we stayed in bed together reading *Phantom* comics. He jokingly referred to me as Lady Diana, Phantom's wife, and to the cars hissing past our window as the whispering grove of Goldenwood, a place where the wind through the trees whispered *Phan...tom...Phan...tom*. Once we went down to Bondi beach and we pretended that it was Keela-Wee with its half pure gold sand and that the Bondi Pavilion was the Jade Hut, a gift from Emperor Joonkoor, the same man who had built the monument of Phantom-Head peak, a gift we duplicated by carving out in the sand a small head of Emo. For a surprise present I sent away for a ring which the Phantom used to leave an impression of a skull on the flesh of his victims. When I gave it to you your face lit up like a child's. You stamped the ring on our toast and we called it 'skull toast' or was it 'phantom toast'? It doesn't matter what it was called, all I knew was that you were happy in going to be a father. Home had also become a sanctuary from the increasingly boring merry-go-round of lectures and talks which soon grow empty as the exile realises that that is all they are — *talk*. At home you were away from your fears of futility and you loved rubbing your hand over my growing belly as if amazed that you were alive to witness this gradual miracle. I felt I had truly become a woman and even Louise's condescending attitude didn't bother me. She was always talking about the sisterhood of women and yet she looked down on me for being pregnant. It was as if I confirmed my primitiveness by being pregnant.

However, for all my initial exhilaration at having a child growing inside me, a curious sense of unease began to overtake me. The first incident that unsettled me concerned Mr Vine, who I really liked because he had been kind to me. His wife left him for a swimming instructor and he became increasingly despondent and lonely. Sometimes he didn't want me to clean the house but only sit and listen to him. He told me about his failing business and his secret infatuation for members of his own sex. One time when I came to clean I found that he had piled up all the precious things in his life (photographs, paintings, jewellery, papers — white people love to preserve things) in the middle of the lounge room and was about to set fire to them. He was drunk and lost and his action reminded me of the stories I had heard about Mister Bacon trying to destroy the most precious thing in his life when he, too, was depressed and drunk. I talked him out of setting fire to his past and helped him to bed where he lay shivering, his eyes glazed as if his heart had finally broken. The following week when I arrived to clean his house I found him lying on a mattress in the lounge room. He was naked and dead. His golden teeth, caught in the morning light, shone brilliantly in his cold mouth. Nearby was a note *Dear Palu, sorry to do this to you, but I knew you would be certain to find me. I don't have any other visitors. Call the police.* At the sight of this dead man I wept and so did my baby inside me. I wondered what taboo this old man had broken in his life to cause himself so much torment. Because I had touched a dead man my baby had too, and I spent the next few days rubbing my body with Coleus leaves to rid it of the stench of death.

However, worse was to come. One afternoon I was looking out my window and I saw a dwarf with red hair and skin like milk walking down the street. I called to Emo but by the time he came the dwarf had vanished. Emo didn't understand my fear of this demon because he belonged to a coastal tribe which didn't know about the evilness of such creatures. They can steal a baby or even kill it in the mother's womb. Over the next few weeks I saw him several times in the street hurrying towards some secret destination but then

117

vanishing before I could see where he was going. He began to haunt my dreams and once I saw him sitting at the bottom of my bed, a small hunched-up creature, chuckling at my fear of him. I knew he wasn't actually there on my bed he was really somewhere in the city thinking of me, penetrating my thoughts. I kept calm by thinking that maybe the demon was on his way to infect other women's wombs. Then Emo left for Melbourne to meet with some exiles and I was left alone. I had asked him not to go but he told me I was being foolish. I panicked when he left and ran to Louise's. She smiled when I told her about the demon. 'There's no such things as demons, Palu.'

'What about Hitler?'

'He was just a man.'

'Then how come he killed millions and millions of people. No, only demons do that, not humans.'

She thought she was so superior to me because she was being logical but she was just a fool. Demons are in every culture. Look at the stained glass windows of Christian churches. In order to calm myself I went to a large department store. I would often spend hours wandering through Sydney's emporiums, imagining I could afford the clothes or furniture on sale. While I was looking at a rack of summer dresses I saw a movement out of the corner of my eye. It was the demon. He vanished amid the racks of clothes but I knew he was searching me out. He had come to kill my child. I hurried down the escalator, clutching my swollen belly, realising I would have to fight the demon alone. As I passed through the food hall I saw him on the other side of the sandwich counter, moving with a determined purpose through the knees of the lunchtime crowd. I looked for other pregnant women, wondering if he might be making for someone else, but there were none. Knowing that if I went to the next escalator he could easily catch me, I retraced my steps and headed back through the cosmetic counters where women wearing beautiful masks of make-up tried to tempt me with perfumes. I was in a real state, sweating profusely and my legs felt spongy and useless. After trying so hard to conceive I was not going to let the demon kill my baby. 'One touch of a red-haired, white-skinned little man is enough to kill any baby,' my mother had told me. As I looked around the glass counters with their glowing bottles of perfume and scents, I remembered how Maz's sister had lost a baby when such a demon had touched her inner thighs. I couldn't see him but I knew he was near because my baby started to spin with fear in my belly. I rushed to the electrical goods department, looking back over my shoulder constantly to make sure he wasn't following me. Dozens of television sets greeted me with images of a spaceman being attacked by green slime on some alien planet. I turned away not wanting to let my guard down and there he was, hurrying through the washing machine section. I made to go the other way but slipped and fell onto the floor. A salesman rushed to help me. I scrambled to my feet to escape but there he was again, rushing towards me. I knew I had to hurt him first. I made a grab for him in the hope of throwing him off. He jumped out of my reach but I lunged for him again and caught him by the shirt collar. 'Hey, let go!' he squeaked.

I shouted at him. 'I'm going to kill you, demon, you've been following me everywhere.'

'Hey, let go you crazy Abo!'

The salesman tried to protect the demon as I swung him back and forth. I was feverish with the anger of fear. The creature squealed like a bat. His voice and eyes told me that he was in league with the bat demon. It took three salesmen and a customer to pull the demon away from me. He refused

119

to lay charges when the police came because he said my pregnancy had caused my 'loony' behaviour but I knew he was scared that if we went to court then the truth would come out.

The demon never appeared again. He didn't have to, he had done his work well. That night I was possessed by an awful giddiness and by the time Emo returned in the morning I was very ill. He took me to hospital where my baby was born dead, the embryo cord wrapped around its throat. The demon had won. I wept all the next day and spat on my cunt and beat it until it was awash with blood and spittle. I cursed myself for not being strong enough to have overcome the evil influence of the demon. Deep down I was possessed by a great, hideous fear that my womb was as dead as the moon. *Say something, Emo, say you still love me. Say 'let's keep trying'. Say it isn't my fault. Blame the demon. You know it was the demon. Don't blame me. Make love to me, don't turn away in bed as if I were death itself. Don't be so silent!*

So great was my shame at having failed that I decided to commit suicide. I went down to the rowing club pier and stood among the empty shoes waiting for myself to jump in. I gazed at my broken, trembling reflection and it seemed that I, too, was all in pieces and that if I had had a baby then I would have been whole. My reflection beckoned me as I leant forward and without knowing I was falling I saw my reflection coming up to greet me like the spirit of my dead self. I hit the water and did not struggle. Unable to swim I sank quickly in the chilly water until my feet touched the warm mud. Spirits began to fight over my body. Hands pulled and tore at me and I was sucked out of the mud and hauled upwards. I hit the air and saw faces peering down at me from the pier. Then I was aware that two men held

120

me in their grasp. I was lifted up onto the pier where a man frantically kissed me while another kneaded me. Soon I was breathing properly and was sitting in the bar of the rowing club, wrapped up in a blanket, drinking a beer. I had been rescued by a rowing team that was returning from practice just as I fell. I pretended it had all been an accident and my smallness and my blackness made it seem that I might do such a silly thing as leaning too far over the pier.

I told Emo nothing about what had happened when he returned from Queensland. I was glad to be alive and regretted having attempted to do something so foolish; suicide is the revenge of cowards. I also realised that my failure to become a mother was because I was still cursed. Although there was nothing I could do to change the fact that I had entered the spirit house, I decided the least I could do was apologise to the birds of paradise. I knew they wanted an apology because I had begun to dream of waking up in a room full of bird of paradise feathers. I had no idea what the dream meant, only that the birds of paradise were thinking of me, so I sought out the only birds I knew existed in Sydney, those in the zoo. At first I couldn't gain their confidence because I had forgotten how to speak to them, but gradually I recalled their language and they began to cluster in front of their cages and talk to me. Amid giggling school children or under the suspicious gaze of the zoo keepers I asked the birds' forgiveness for what my father and I had done to their cousins. Their forgiveness didn't come easily. They are a proud and stubborn bird and they wanted me to be truly apologetic. They said to me *you will know you have been truly forgiven when you wake up and your room is filled with our feathers.*

Their words gave me new spirit because they brought a sense of hope. And this was shown by the way Emo started to make love to me again. We made love in positions in which all his semen could be kept inside me. Gradually happiness returned to me and with it the belief that I would have a child next time.

The third year into our exile Emo became spokesman for all exiles. As the government back home grew more corrupt and vicious, so the number of exiles fleeing the country grew larger. Our flat became a halfway house for many on arrival in Australia, and I grew used to these wide-eyed people sitting as if mesmerised before the television, amazed at the world they now found themselves in. The network of exiles expanded throughout Australia and Emo was away more often than he was home, and I was glad I had a job with which to fill the empty hours. When he was home Emo often visited the Andrews to seek advice from Ted who, I knew, would give it copiously and endlessly and in a very boring fashion, so I stayed away. Where was that cocky girl from the plantation and the teachers' college? She was at home waiting for her belly to bloom again. Less confident of myself I became content to drift through my days as if I were part of a daydream rather than the dreamer.

Dreams have been preoccupying me lately. I have asked the governor if I may be allowed to walk in the compound of an evening when everyone else is back in their cells or barracks. I know that if I ask to walk at a time when no one else can talk to me then perhaps permission will be granted. In the far corner of the compound is a rockpile which is being used to build the new cell block and I may be able to find there what I am looking for and, if I can, then I may be able to defeat you. I wonder how much time I have to do that? Last night I woke up when I heard my gecko wheezing — whenever he does that I know he is afraid. I opened my eyes and saw him perched on the wall, almost a hand's reach away. He had never been so close to me before. Perhaps, I thought, he had ventured that close to me because he was scared that I might have died in my sleep. His black eyes shone brightly, caught in the moonlight. I followed his gaze and saw someone staring at me through the small grating in the cell door. The eye was curious and unblinking as if it had been staring at me for some time. I recognised it, it was the governor. Was he imagining me dead? Or was he silently cursing me for being such a burden to him? Once he realised I recognised him his eye blinked and disappeared. The gecko stopped wheezing and stared at me in silence. He, too, had recognised the governor and had been warning me. I wanted to reach out and feel his velvet skin and beating heart but I knew that even a half-hearted grab for him would send him fleeing. As he looked at me, with that curious near grin on his face, I wondered if he ever dreamt and would we ever share the same dream?

After my miscarriage I grew distracted and difficult to be with. I began to hate Australia. It was nothing like the country I had thought it would be. It was too noisy and too aggressive. I felt as if I were even succumbing to the heavy, polluted air. Some days passed without me being aware that I had actually lived them. These feelings were made worse by Emo's absences interstate to attend meetings and try to maintain the enthusiasm of fellow exiles. As I thought of him in my lonely bed I began to imagine that he was being unfaithful. I could not shake off this thought. I knew he was attractive to white women; I was not stupid, I had seen the way they looked at his body — a white woman's lust is naked and obvious (I had even seen Louise staring at him, admiring his black beauty). I knew that white women were intrigued by his colour just as white men were attracted by my blackness. One man, Mr Cornwell, whose house I cleaned after Mr Vine's death, openly stared at me and one day as I was dusting the record cabinet he had put his hand on my bum, saying, 'How about it, Palu, want a bit of fun?' I had slapped his hand away but he had not been in the least apologetic. 'I've never had a black girl before.'

'I will tell Mrs Cornwell if you touch me like that again.'

He had been annoyed for a moment, like a child who has been denied a sweet, but then he had shrugged and walked away as if it meant nothing. I had had other men rub up against me in crowded buses. They always smiled as if I, a black woman, were somehow of looser morals than a white woman and would, as Australians say, 'come across' at the merest whisper of a touch.

My jealousy would sometimes get the better of me and I would ask Emo if he had other women while he was away. He would laugh and call me foolish and yet, as time went on, I began to suspect he was having an affair. I saw a distant gaze in his eyes when he looked at me and for the first time he began to grow terse with me, giving me the impression that everything I said was stupid and not worth listening to. One time when we were making love he rubbed my belly in a way he had not before, as if he were fondling the flesh of another woman. One night, not long afterwards, he came home late and as he slipped into bed beside me I smelt a woman's perfume on his cheek and neck. I shook him, demanding to know who he was sleeping with. He grew angry, finding my jealousy irrational. He told me that a drunken white woman had kissed him goodbye at a meeting she had attended with her husband. I knew my jealous outburst was silly and I vowed not to be childish again. I tried to tell myself that my highly strung emotions were part of my sense of failure at being a mother and also my general disaffection with Australia and its heartlessness. But I could not get rid of the awful feeling that he was having an affair.

My major consolation during that period was the newly arrived exiles who came with stories of what was happening back home and with each story it seemed, for a moment at least, that the end to our exile was approaching. It was one of those new arrivals who, when talking about the mass jailings of the regime's critics, mentioned that in some parts of the Highlands coffee had been attacked by a fungal disease. The implications of this bypassed both him and Emo.

'It's going to destroy the economy,' I said, overhearing the conversation. They turned to where I stood in the doorway.

'What do you mean?' said Emo.

'There is no way to stop rust, unless you can spray the crops eight or ten times a year. Rust is so quick that in a few months the whole crop will be gone.' I then talked about the various coffee diseases and how to prevent them.

They began to understand the consequences. A destroyed coffee industry could destroy the government.

The exile was clearly impressed by my knowledge and asked me where I had learnt so much. Emo answered for me: 'Palu used to work on a coffee plantation.'

It amused me to think that he was still jealous of my relationship with Mister Bacon and could not even mention it now.

'You picked up quite a lot of information about coffee then?'

'Oh, yes. Coffee pickers pick up more than you think.'

Emo gave me a look, warning me by his expression not to be too funny or clever. I took my cue and, pleased with myself, went back to preparing dinner, little realising that the coffee crop would be devastated in an even shorter time than I had predicted. That night I dreamt of Mister Bacon crying amid his blighted coffee bean bushes.

Nambweapa'w took me out for a walk in the compound this evening. I could feel hundreds of eyes peering at me through cell windows as I slowly made my way around the square. When we came to the rockpile I paused, as if tired, and sat on a large boulder. As I inspected the rocks around me, trying to find one I could use, Nambweapa'w gazed at the faces staring at me from the distance.

'Do you realise they all hate you?'

'Yes.'

'So why did you want to come out here? So you can taunt them?'

'I just wanted a walk, that's all.'

'Come on, I don't like this, we're going inside.'

'The governor said ten minutes.'

'It's been more than ten minutes.'

I was annoyed at not having had enough time to find my stone but realised I had best obey him or else I might not get another chance to find what I was looking for.

'Another woman would be ashamed to flaunt herself like you,' he said as he walked me inside. 'Your behaviour will only confirm that you are a witch.'

'I am,' I said, smiling, tired of being called one. He stopped and looked at me in the dingy corridor and I saw that familiar expression of desire and fear in his eyes. Despite his best intentions his manhood became erect. I laughed at his expanding trouser crutch. He spat on me, hating me for making him want me so much. Surprised at his own reaction he roughly wiped the spit from my neck. I said nothing because I knew he was scared that I would tell the governor what he had done. I was untouchable until my execution.

'We'll have a walk in the compound again tomorrow?'

He nodded and silently took me to my cell.

To celebrate our three years in exile the Andrews decided to take Emo and I (as if it were some marvellous anniversary) on a tour of the Art Gallery and then have lunch in the Botanical Gardens. It was one of those glorious Sydney spring days. I felt better than I had for a long time. My heart was full of love for Emo and I could feel the semen he had put inside me just a few hours before. It was therefore strange to be walking beside Ted who had made himself sterile because he thought children 'had no part in the madness of the present world situation'. I tried to stay an arm's reach away from him as we walked to the gallery, not wanting his sterile touch to infect my womb. When I had heard about his vasectomy it had made him less of a man to me and all his political talk now seemed trivial as if I were hearing the words of half a man.

When we got to the gallery we separated. Emo, carefree and happy, went off with Ted to look at a collection of photographs illustrating the exploitation of sugarcane cutters in Queensland, while Louise showed me Australian art. She knew a lot about everything and explained the paintings as if I were one of her students. We stopped in front of one of her favourites, a portrait of two sisters languishing on a sofa in long white dresses. 'The artist died young. He was one of the few male painters of that time who knew how to paint women...' she lectured. But as she went on I began to tune out. Something else began to overwhelm me. It was the smell of dead roses and a woman on heat. I looked at Louise. Her cheeks were flushed and the armpits of her dress were wet. She was a woman on heat. And the smell of dead roses rising from her skin — I had smelt that perfume before; on Emo. It struck me, with a terrible force, that the woman standing next to me had been sleeping with my husband. Devastated, I could not move as she wandered on to the next painting, her mouth opening and closing but no words entering my ears. Realising I was not beside her she turned to me, her face showing concern.

'Are you all right, Palu? You look ill.'

'I have to go to the dunny,' I heard myself say and a moment later I found myself standing at the top of a stairwell. My mind was filled with hideous images of Emo and Louise making love. I wanted to be sick. I do not remember going down the stairs. One moment I was at the top, the next I was at the bottom as if I had been swallowed up by the basement. All those times I had seen them talking together or just standing next to each other haunted me with my new interpretation of them. I wandered through the semi-darkness of the basement. My body had taken control and my mind had gone into a state of panic. It is as if you are listening to me now and are mocking that moment and your face is coming down the corridor like a slow whirlwind of craziness, calling for sacrifice, and I hear that familiar voice, 'Men have a craze for pig flesh, just as they have for justice and revenge and I am crazed for all three' and I want, I want you to shut up and get out of my head and I am trying to push you out but there you are in a frenzy of lust with Louise and I cannot rid myself of you. I stopped in front of a glass cabinet, my brain full of confusion. For a time I did not realise what was before me and then my eyes focused and I saw creatures staring at me. Before me were the gods and spirits of a men's spirit house; alligator ghosts, bat demons, ibis spirits and guardians of the flutes. Frozen in wood they glared at me. Their leader, a bat demon, had a smile as large as an alligator's mouth and a penis as big as a spear. Memories of breaking the taboo of the spirit house when I was a child rushed back to me. I felt as if I had fallen into a nightmare. What was real? Emo and Louise having an affair or this cabinet of spirits? I did not know, except that before me was a pack of demons. They were not dead, only pretending to be and waiting for a chance to rule again. Didn't the white collectors realise that those smiles on the demons' faces were smiles of triumph because the demons knew the wood was only make believe. The demons began to move. The smiles turned into grins and the limbs began to writhe with life. The alligator demon pressed its face against the glass. Saliva dripped from its teeth as it savoured the idea of devouring me. Paralysed with fright I could not move and then the glass began to crack.

I fainted and when I awoke I found myself confronted by curious faces peering down at me. I looked around and saw that I was in an office of the gallery and Emo, Ted and Louise were there, full of concern. The art gallery manager asked me if I was feeling better. My mind was still full of the demons.

'They are only pretending to be dead.'

'Who?'

'The carvings in the glass boxes.'

'My wife is a very superstitious woman,' Emo said. He was annoyed at me for embarrassing him. *I'm glad I embarrassed you because I hate you, I hate you for betraying me with that slut.*

I lied and said I was feeling fine and so we went off on our picnic in the Botanical Gardens. A peculiar emotion gripped me; a euphoria that made me feel as if I were floating with the clouds, looking down on everything below. Watching Louise pass sandwiches to Emo, as if he were just a casual

friend, I felt I had a power over them. *I knew the truth!*
I made fun of myself, calling myself a primitive who loved
Dickens. Louise laughed and I laughed with her, knowing
I would have the last laugh. I gazed down on Ted, too. He
was so stupid that he did not know what was happening
between his wife and Emo. This strange euphoria made me
rise above the hurt and bitterness I felt, especially towards
Louise who, even as she sat eating her picnic lunch, talked
of how women should be 'sisters'. She rubbed her belly after
only one sandwich and said, 'I'm full, I don't know how
you can eat so much, Palu.' A yodelling sweetheart out of
the belly of a whore. Your yodel will infect the air and it
will whirl down the corridors of this prison like an evil wind.

The euphoria grew so strong that I thought I would vomit.
I needed to escape from Emo and Louise so I pretended
I was going to feed the ducks. I left the trio talking about
rumours of a coup back home (always rumours, always second-
hand information, always ridiculous hopes raised then
crushed). At the pond the euphoria vanished as quickly as
it had arrived. I wept. I was in exile not only from my country
but also from my husband. How long would I have to pay
for having broken the taboos in my childhood? I wept until
I was empty. I then grew angry and decided to confront
the two about their affair. As I was about to return I heard
children squealing with delight and saw a black swan running
across the lawns after a frog. The swan eventually gave up
the chase and returned to the lotus-filled pond. The frog
came towards me and I caught it. Gazing into its large wet
eyes I knew it had been sent to me by a spirit. I hid it
in my frock and returned to the picnic where the trio was
anxiously waiting for me.

'We were very worried about you, Palu,' said Louise.

I looked her in the eye and smiled. She shifted uneasily on the grass. 'There was no need to be, Louise.'

Thinking that my moods were the result of a continuing preoccupation with my miscarriage the three took me to Luna Park. It was as if they were trying to jolly a child. On the wild rides they screamed with terrified delight, I screamed out in despair at being exiled from you. I wanted to hate you but all my thoughts were taken up with revenge against Louise.

That night while Emo slept I gathered up a handful of ashes from the fireplace and sneaked outside. I hurried along to the Andrews' house. Dogs barked at me as I passed along the suburban streets; they knew I was going to destroy someone. Dogs originate from shit and if you let a dog know that you are aware of its origins then it will be afraid of you. I glared at the Andrews' German Shepherd and it cowered and came to me with its tail between its legs. I took off my dress and rubbed the ashes over my body. I then rubbed sprigs of herbs I had collected up my cunt until they were awash with blood. I wiped the bloody herbs on the front and back doorsteps so that when Louise passed over the blood she would be rendered frigid by my power. I tied a piece of string around the frog's stomach and fastened the end of the string to a stick which I rammed into the earth under a large hydrangea near the side of the house. I spoke a curse over it and in the curse I asked that Louise never fuck my Emo again and that she die alone and unloved. I spent three days wondering if my magic had worked; if I returned and the frog had escaped that meant that Louise had escaped the magic. On the third night I went back and the frog was still there, dying and sick; just as Louise would soon be.

The magic began to work. I heard that she was ill and frequently vomiting. I made a love potion out of plants which I stole from the exotic section of the Botanical Gardens. I mixed them in with Emo's food and fed them to him. I also put my pubic hairs in his cigarettes. Gradually his tenderness and love for me returned.

As the crisis worsened back home his reliance on Ted began to lessen. Reports of the spread of the fungus began to appear in Australian newspapers. The nation's coffee crop was on its way to being totally destroyed and, as if symptomatic of the government's corruption, the entire sugar crop was also attacked by a mysterious fungus. This period in our history was called 'The Time of the Fungus'. The government could do nothing but watch impotently as its two cash crops for the international market disappeared. Unrest was reported from every province and calls for the government's overthrow grew more persistent. Our consul in Sydney secretly visited Emo and asked whether he would become part of the government. Emo, realising he was now in a position of strength, said he would return only to head an entirely new government. Reports began to appear in our newspapers about Emo, calling him that 'crazy agitator' and 'leftish radical' who was too afraid to return but hid in Australia like some dog. Such articles only made Emo seem more important. Stop that woman! Stop that singing! I can't concentrate. Why don't those fools turn down the radio. This morning the governor addressed the prisoners in the compound. He wanted to introduce himself to those who will soon die but the loudspeaker system wasn't working properly; somehow it had been wrongly connected to the radio. Instead of hearing his platitudes the prisoners heard singing from the radio. And there was the fat fool seeming to be miming, in a girl's voice:

I have come from far away
To see my loved one today
Oh, let my boy be there
Or I'll cry a lonesome tear

In another context it would be funny but here there was
no laughter, only the fear that the governor's public humiliation would result in more deaths. Her yodel is still going,
echoing down the corridor, like a dying demon crying for
revenge. My gecko is grimacing, the yodel hurts even his
ears. I will write to shut out her singing.

I am back at The Time of the Fungus and people are rioting
in the towns, even in the backlands, demanding that the
government do something about the fungus. Its answer was
bloodshed and violent repression. It was as if the fungus
had attacked the minds of men as well. As each new report
of unrest and massacre came in Emo and his fellow exiles
gloated; I learnt a valuable lesson in politics — one man's
disaster is another man's triumph. The Time of the Fungus
was soon to become The Time of Emoti. Representatives
of the various political factions flew to Australia to try and
convince Emo to join their side. What he wanted, however,
was the support of the army, because he needed it to take
over the government. But the army saw him as leftwing,
even communist. However, Emo had one great power —
he was one of the few potential leaders seen as being incorruptible and it was not long before our diseased country called
him to come and rescue it.

The yodelling has stopped and been replaced by sombre music.
I know that music, so does everyone here. There is to be
an announcement of some death. Are you dead? No, I can

feel your presence emanating from the palace and it is chilling me to the bone. You are thinking of me; is my death to be announced?

Nambweapa'w came in, almost catching me writing this. He pretended interest in my bed, wanting to know if it is strong enough. I said it was but what he really wanted from me was a promise not to tell the governor that he had spat on me. Every time he looked at me I looked away. He is nervy, too, waiting to see what the announcement will be. To keep calm I go on writing.

At the Time of the Fungus the Andrews separated, for what reason I did not know at the time. Louise went to live in Melbourne without saying goodbye. Ted began to appear at our flat looking forlorn and lost. His position and his apprentice's were now reversed; Ted had always been able to talk brilliantly about politics but Emo was now preparing to actually take part in them. As more exiles crowded into our lounge room to discuss the return home, Ted began to vanish into the background, a useless lost white face amid a sea of black faces until, eventually, he didn't even bother to join the discussions but stayed in the kitchen, as lost there as he was in the lounge room. He had obviously discovered that Emo had had an affair with Louise and it irritated me that he accepted the situation so meekly. White men began to seem very weak to me and I was amused at how easy it was for me to order Ted around, like some sort of menial. There was no light left in his eyes. He was a living dead man, whereas Emo was full of energy and purpose.

I knew that the time for our return was near when Emo bought a new angel. He had bought it from a stone mason's workshop that specialised in headstones. It was almost the size of a human and was made of marble. Emo placed it in the centre of all his other angels. This was *the* angel which would protect him from harm. It was beautiful, with a calm, reassuring smile, wings that curved up from its back like a bird in flight and hands as delicate as a white woman's. Looking at it made me realise just how great was Emo's anxiety. That confidence and assurance which he showed to others hid a great fear. Again that curious mixture in him; fear and resolve. Resolve to go ahead with actions but also fear at the result of such actions. Where did fear and resolve end and begin? Only the angel knew and only it heard your silent prayers. Your fear and resolve must be so great now that only a stone angel, hundreds of feet high, would be capable of listening to your prayers.

I have found *you*. Nambweapa'w allowed me to search through the rockpile this evening to my heart's content. 'I think you're going mad,' he said, as I inspected stones in the fading light, trying to pay no attention to the prisoners hissing at me from their cell windows. 'What are you searching for, Mrs President?'

'Something to keep me company.'

Just as it was getting almost too dark to see I came upon what I knew I would. I asked Nambweapa'w if I could keep it in my cell. His tongue clicked like a cricket and he shook his head. 'You're really a crazy woman.'

'Please,' I begged.

'You might use it as a weapon.'

I laughed. 'On the guards? You must be joking.'

'But why do you want it?'

'It'll make me less lonely.'

You are now before me as I write. Both the gecko and

I recognise you. The stone is about the size of my hand. The front of it is a jumble of bumps. When I turn it to the side then you appear. There is no mistaking it. It is *your* profile. I have found my dreamstone of you. See, the corridor light has caught your stony profile and it is easy to recognise your high brow, half triangle, almost Western nose and sensuous mouth. It is the profile I remember from the time when you were in your angel room after the news came that the army would support you if you went back. You did not hear me when I came home from cleaning and the door to the angel room was open. Now that it was certain you were about to return you were preparing to confront your fear, like a young tribesman preparing to duel for the chiefdom.

After rubbing his cock to erection Emo picked up a small green stem of some herb. It had barbs pointing slightly upward along its length and, with a shudder that ran visibly through his thighs and torso, he inserted it deep down the hole of his penis and then yanked it out. The barbs caught and tore the inside lining of his penis. Blood oozed from the opening. He repeated the action three or four times until blood spurted out, a fine spray of it covering the feet and dress of the angel. Groaning with agony he used eight stems five or six times each until the barbs wore off and the blood stopped flowing. I could barely stop myself from crying out, telling him to stop but if I had he would never have forgiven me. After using up all his stems he picked up a razor blade which he had broken into a sharp point. He rubbed his penis erect again, peeled back the foreskin and began to jab violently at the head of it until it, too, sprayed blood. He had achieved what he wanted to. His desire for power had conquered his fear of physical pain. And in conquering this fear he had also conquered the fear of failure that had haunted him. His profile was calm and beautiful; like my dreamstone.

The news has just come through. Three cabinet ministers perished in the Highlands when their plane crashed into a mountain. The announcer said it was a terrible accident. It was no accident. You made that plane crash and with it went the only three ministers who ever represented a threat to you. There is only one threat left and it is here, gazing at your stone profile. You think that you will come to me tonight in my dreams and scare me shitless but I will come to you first, entering this stone night after night until you are afraid to dream.

Our return home had to be kept secret so we travelled by cruise ship to the holiday islands just off our eastern coast. Pretending to be tourists, and under an alias (Mr and Mrs Dickens, a surname which you indulged me in because you were concerned about more pressing things), we nervously feigned relaxed enjoyment while old people basked on the sundeck like corpses mummifying in the sun and young people partied all night, frantically seeking a bed partner before dawn.

The evening before we were to leave the ship we stood together on the bow watching home invisibly approach. Nearby a young couple drunkenly groped one another openly and without embarrassment. An old man came up to us and said loudly, 'You two seem to be a bit out of it.' Emo flinched as if our secret had been discovered but the old man only had a lonely desire for talk. Anyway, he was right, we were out of it. Having spent three years in Australia I had forgotten just how odd Emo and I must have looked on this holiday ship filled with whites desperately seeking pleasure. The old man recognised in our features where we had been born and told us how he had run a sugar cane plantation there right up until independence. 'I hear the place has gone to seed now,' he said, gazing at it lying somewhere beyond the dark horizon. 'Such a shame, it used to be a marvellous country.'

'It will be again,' said Emo, speaking for the first time, his face beautiful in the rainbow cast by the fairy lights that ran along the deck. I could see that, as we drew closer to home, his sense of mission and purpose were becoming part of him. Having passed his own painful initiation test in the angel room he now could not turn back. The old man smiled. Did he know what Emo was about to embark upon? It was hard to tell in the dim light but I did see, as the old man went on talking about his love for our country, how much it had ingrained itself into his being.

Indeed, I had forgotten how much it was a part of me until, when we were on an army boat, I saw the coast and began to cry. I had not truly known how much I had missed my homeland. Emo, homesick too, put his arm around my waist in a rare gesture of public affection, as the mountains rose up out of the sea. *Ripperty Kye A-hoo!* my heart sang out; I am back home!

When we came ashore we were met by some army officers who immediately took Emo aside to talk about their plans for taking over the government. Left alone I walked into the nearby jungle as night fell. It smelt of blooming flowers, trees, rot and fertility, as if even night could not stop its violent ardour. How can I describe to you, Mr Gecko, you who have probably never heard the sounds of the jungle, because on this barren island you hear only screams, groans and the whispers of faint hope, the song of an animal that is like a man yodelling with joy or the creaking tendons of an owl's wing as it passes within a breath of you? Then there are all those sounds of unknown animals and insects that fill your ears with a musical dissonance of clearing throats, creaking groans and rasping cries and, rippling through this is an undercurrent of mysterious noises; click-clacking, tsks, hissing, whispering, whishing and humming. I stood, transfixed, as all around me ghosts, animals, spirits and night birds fought, haunted and loved one another in the noisy night. I had come home, my exile was over!

When I returned to the beach Emo was by himself, staring out to sea, withdrawn and thoughtful. He heard my squeaky footsteps on the sand and turned around, glad to see me.

'What is going to happen?'

'The government refuses to resign.'

This came as a shock because we had been led to believe that all the army had to do was to say it would overthrow the government, if it did not agree to its own demise, for it to capitulate. Politicians, however, are the same everywhere; they will never willingly give up power. The people hated it, even some ministers hated being part of such an inept, corrupt government, but still the President and his cronies would not accept the inevitable. As we walked along the beach Emo told me how the army intended to scare the government into resigning by putting on a show of force. I wanted to believe that this was all that would happen, just as Emo did. His great fear was coming to power over a mountain of corpses.

Immersed in talking about what the government would do (once we did talk like this, once you treated me as your equal) we walked for a long time until we were kilometres from the camp. We stopped when we realised how far we had gone and, meaning to return, we turned around to retrace our steps only to stop when we caught the longing in each other's eyes. I knew he saw in me the young woman whom he had fallen in love with at college and I saw in him the handsome young man who, lit by the moonlit ocean, gave me his cigarette filled with love magic. Returning from exile had renewed us both. We made love on the warm sand and slept in each other's arms until the morning tide, like some cold, wet tongue, licked us awake. Mr Gecko, you are sniggering, believe me, this is not me parroting some official legend — if only that were so — no, Emo was once a man capable of love.

Like a precious bundle we were shunted from village to village over the next two weeks, staying only a short time in one place so as to avoid capture. The army, we soon found out, wasn't unified in its support for Emo. The younger troops, led by a Night Person, Colonel Akwanaamae, supported him but the older troops, who had spent most of their lives under the colonial government, and were therefore conservative, opposed Emo, believing he was a communist. As we hurried from village to village, moving carefully along obscure jungle paths, we saw the effects of The Time of the Fungus with our own eyes. Plantations and small village plots of coffee bushes were destroyed, the leaves withered and tortured by the fungus. The sugar cane stalks had been made so frail that a child's hand could crush them into dust. It was easy to see why so many people supported Emo, he was their one hope to stop this evil. At each village people came out to greet us, having heard of this legendary man who had come back home from across the sea to save them. They waited patiently for our arrival, wearing arse grass, their faces yellow or red (the colours of greeting a great warrior or ancestor), and slapped their sides and clicked their tongues in excitement when we appeared. An evil was upon them and only a warrior returning from the underworld could defeat it.

Emo grew tired of this life on the run and wanted to go to the capital and force the President to resign but even he knew, deep down, that it was too dangerous. 'I feel like a boy who is supposed to be chief but is not allowed into the spirit house,' he would say. I was glad that Colonel Akwanaamae kept Emo away from the capital because I knew there would be violence. There I am, Emo, watching you as you sleep on the dirt floor of the chief's hut that was always given to us, and I am scared that even our guard of thirty soldiers may not be enough to stop us from being killed in our sleep. Do not be impatient, Emo, I am whispering *wait!* it will not take long. I know because all the signs are there; a star falls from the sky at the same time every night and there are no bats obscuring the moon. I watch you, proud and apprehensive, your sperm inside me, desperately wanting your child, the child of a great man. It is a lie for the newspapers to say, Mr Gecko, that I tried to dissuade Emo from becoming President during this time. I admit I am a coward but I wasn't going to stand in the way of his destiny.

Then the call came; the army rebels had won and Emo was asked to form a government. Remember, my stonehead, how you tried to be calm when you heard the news over the crackling radio headphones, but when I congratulated you with a hug your body was rigid with excitement.

Only when we neared the capital did we hear the stories of soldiers fighting one another and of the murder of civilians. Yet Port Andrews seemed unscarred and thousands of people lined the roadside to wave at their new President. On the steps of the palace, as if he were a real estate salesman waiting to hand over a property, stood Colonel Akwanaamae. He saluted and said, grinning, 'Welcome President Emoti!' That grin! It was the grin of a barbarian. Remember how we sat together in the back seat of the former President's armed car as we drove to the football ground a few hours later for your inauguration, and how Colonel Akwanaamae turned around in the front seat and proudly told us that after his troops had taken over the barracks of the opposing army faction, they had invaded the palace and after much searching had found the President cowering in the bathroom as if hiding from some jealous husband? 'Will you resign?' Colonel Akwanaamae is supposed to have asked. Whatever the President replied made no difference because the Colonel strangled him. 'I did it for you, President Emoti,' he said, as you recoiled from this jovial Night Person with his yellow teeth and crimson gums shining with pleasure at the memory of his deed. Your great fear had been well-founded; you did come to power on the corpses of others and although you soon forgot about it the stain was impossible to remove. Later, whenever Colonel Akwanaamae was in my presence a shiver ran down my back. He saw my dread and would say, with that broad grin, 'Palu, how are you, am I disturbing you?' He would tease me by making a gesture towards me as if to touch me with his huge, calloused hands and I would flinch, imagining my throat being squeezed between them as I struggled for air, and my final vision being of his grin of exertion. I think of you often, Colonel Akwanaamae, wondering if you will be my executioner. I have imagined my death at your hands so often recently that it would not surprise me if it did happen.

Emo had wondered what the price of the army supporting him would be and the answer was there in Colonel Akwanaamae; he became a general and Minister for the Army. The army became an indisputable part of the government

142

and those troops who had not supported the coup were demoted or forced to resign or, as some stories had it, murdered. Yet for all Akwanaamae's ruthlessness he, like his troops, did want Emo to succeed; the nation was in crisis.

Suddenly, and for no apparent reason, I have been interrogated. A few hours ago some guards burst into my cell. I barely had time to hide these pages. They picked me up and escorted me to the governor's office. Nambweapa'w was with them. I looked to him for some sign as to what was going to happen to me but he turned away, pretending he did not know me. I was ushered into the office and saw the governor sitting to the side of his desk. Behind the desk sat Larenkeni, head of the Secret Police. Of all the ministers apart from Colonel Akwanaamae, he is the only one to have survived the years of Emoti's rule. He has too much information on everybody to be thrown aside. Like Akwanaamae he gave his total allegiance to the President because Emo had allowed Night People to take part in the running of the government for the first time.

I knew that there must be something serious afoot if Larenkeni had travelled all this way. He was uncomfortable talking to me and shifted uneasily in his chair. He tried to seem detached but this was a difficult situation for him. There I was, the President's wife and a woman whom he had, I know, liked greatly. At receptions and parties he had always made sure he talked to me, telling me his awful jokes and trying to pretend that his job was something akin to being the Minister for Finance rather than a man who arranged tortures and who had, I now know, designed this island of pain in the middle of the jungle. Knowing he was uneasy I decided to take advantage of it.

'What is this about?'

He shuffled through a few papers and glanced, unconsciously, at the photograph of my husband, unable to look me in the face. I looked at your eyes, Emo; they are dead. The retoucher had tried to put life into them but they still look like the eyes of a cooked fish.

'Just a few questions, Palu.'

'Mrs President,' I corrected him, arrogant in my nervousness.

He grimaced and looked across at the governor as if seeking an explanation for my behaviour. The governor shrugged as if to say *she's always like this*. I silently asked him *why are you here? Have you come to kill me?* In order to deal with me he took on the air of a professional interrogator and began to ask me questions from a prepared list.

'Do you have any complaints about your treatment here?'

The governor squirmed slightly, waiting for my answer. I thought of criticising him but realised nothing would be gained.

'No.'

Both men were pleased that I was not going to complain; I had made things easy for them.

'I want to ask you a few questions so as to clarify some matters.'

'Before you do — I want to know why I am here.'

He looked at me stonily, it was an expression I imagine many prisoners had seen as they were interrogated by Larenkeni in the special cells of the Secret Police.

'I will do the asking and you will answer.'

Even the governor was unnerved by his coldness. I glanced at the dead eyes of my husband staring down at me like some alien from another planet and realised why he and Larenkeni get on so well; they have created images of themselves that are no longer human; they have evolved into figureheads that have no emotion. Dependent on one another they have created a darkness as deep and as insidious as soot running through veins.

'It's time you confessed.'

'Confessed to what?'

'Everything, Mrs Emoti. You realise, of course, that people regard you as the main opposition to the President.'

'The prisoners here don't.'

He went silent and examined his questions, then looked back up at me. 'Do you like the President?'

The question stunned me. It was too personal and yet not personal enough. I looked at the photograph on the wall to remind myself of who I should talk about; President Emoti or Emo.

'I used to love him.'

Larenkeni's lips tightened. He had been unprepared for such a personal answer. He pushed on. 'So you hate him?'

'I hate what he's become.'

The answer satisfied him. He could deal with hate.

'In hating him you wanted to overthrow him?'

I laughed. 'Overthrow my husband? I just wanted him to become more human. I didn't want to overthrow him. I wanted him to see what he had become.'

'And what has he become?'

I shrugged, not wanting to convict myself.

'A monster? A tyrant? Dictator? What words do you think would describe him?'

'You seem to know them all. Perhaps you should choose.'

Too smart by half, Palu, I thought to myself as he returned to his sheet. There was something inept about his questioning which I found strange, as if he were flitting from topic to topic out of some uneasiness with this duty, or had I not understood the subtle method of his interrogation? Then, as he slowly scanned the questions, I suddenly recognised the handwriting. Even upside down I knew that writing — it was Emo's! He had written questions for Larenkeni to ask me. This has become our final method of communication.

Larenkeni went on, asking me questions in a more relentless fashion, giving me hardly any time to reflect on my answers. After a time I realised where all this was leading; I was supposed to condemn myself as President Emoti's would-be assassin. I tried not to. Finally, towards the end of the interrogation, Larenkeni came straight out and asked me if I had intended to kill you. I hated you at that moment. Perhaps hate is not a strong enough word. I *loathed* you for having written that question for him to ask. I *loathed* your cowardice and your paranoia.

'It's a lie. I did not want to kill him. You know that.'

He looked away, knowing that it was a truly monstrous lie. He pulled a typewritten page out from under the hand-written question sheet and handed it to me. 'I want you to read and sign it, Mrs Emoti.'

It was a confession. In it I said that I had wanted to overthrow the President and kill him but before I could fully put the plan into operation I had been caught redhanded making a concoction of leaves to slowly paralyse him. I wanted to laugh at the confession's outrageous fiction but all I could do was feel an intense, all-consuming loathing for you, Emo. You have become the Emperor of Darkness and you must be destroyed.

I handed back the confession. 'I won't sign it because it's not true.'

'If you sign it then you can go free.'

I smiled, even he didn't believe what he had said. 'If I sign it then I sign my death warrant. If I confess then his conscience is clear, he can then kill me. To kill me he is going to have to dirty his hands. If he wasn't such a coward he would kill me himself.'

I began to feel better. I now knew that Emo was scared of me and that he felt uneasy about what he had done. I was still an open wound. I will enter that bloody sore and destroy you.

Larenkeni pondered the unsigned confession. The stony expression changed. He was now a friend trying to talk sense to someone who was being childish. 'You must sign it, Palu. It will be easier for you. Once you sign it then this prison will be just a memory.'

'You'll have to report back to him that your mission was unsuccessful. You can tell my husband that the prison has done wonders for my figure.'

'You are just one of many in this prison,' he said maliciously, 'and you will be treated as the assassin you really are. Good afternoon, Mrs Emoti.'

Larenkeni's presence at the prison is unnerving everyone. Many of the prisoners remember his brutal interrogations in the police cells. Rumours are flying thick and fast and people are frightened, believing that he has come to oversee the final extermination. Other rumours criticise me, saying that if only I had signed the confession then everyone could go free. The guards are scared too and they patrol the corridors relentlessly and methodically, peeking in at me at all sorts of odd moments. No one wants to be in Larenkeni's bad books. It is difficult to get enough time to write because of the close attention I am getting while he is here.

My main purpose is to get to you. The moonlight is caressing the dreamstone. The stone is softening before my eyes. Your profile is becoming skin and bone and blood. Your eyes are losing their blankness and the emerging pupils move to look at me. The gecko is crying out in alarm from deep in his hiding place. Your voice floats down the corridor like some deadly gas:

'Dear Friends, you have lifted the morale of the man who directs the destiny of our nation so as to signify to him that his mission, his important mission, has just begun. But someone is trying to stop it, that someone is a person, is a group, and they are using youth, the fine flower of youth for shameful purposes. The power I have from you, the power I have from you alone, no power in this world can take away from me, can stop me from fulfilling my mission. Lizards have come out from under rocks and are using youths to help them. Dear friends, I know those lizards, I know where they are, who they are and where they hide... There are some people, some backward people who can think only of destruction... They have become mad...'

Those stone lips move in time with your voice. You are entering my dreams tonight as I enter yours. I can already picture you returning from the radio station. The car moves through the silent streets. I am not put off by the second car you use to fool would-be assassins. No, I can sense your car and it is moving down Tege street towards the palace while the false one, with your false shadow inside it, winds its way past the docks. A guard opens the car door and President Emoti silently moves up the palace steps. Everywhere silence; only hands opening doors or saluting. You peek in at the sleeping white Princess of Darkness. Rake thin and self-satisfied, even in sleep, her mind is conceiving another dead tune. Moving on you arrive at your own bedroom. The black suit weighs as much as another man clinging to your body. Empty of happiness you slip in between the sheets, your body still that of a black prince. I can feel your eyes closing and you are about to dream. It is time that I went to sleep to dream of you and like a snake I will wind my way into the narrowest crevice that leads into your starless mind.

Last night I slept beside you. Your sleep was restless and you mumbled things. I heard my name and knew your dreams were of me. You want me to die so you can be free of me. Once you woke in the middle of a dream, sensing I was beside you. You switched on the bedside lamp but I was not there, yet for months you have never felt my presence so close to you. Am I delirious, you thought; even the bed smells of Palu. I saw your face and its intimate details, details only love or dreams can provide; there are the lines under your eyes, the whites are clouded with faint lines of red veins and your breath is hoarse, the sort of breathing that comes before an illness. Bubbles of sweat cover your handsome lifeless face as you stare at my side of the bed. Thirteen years ago your face was confident and alive. You *were* my black prince then.

Everyone marvelled at President Emoti's energy in the early days. He had inherited a country that was known for its laziness and a nation that was at a loss as to its future. Port Andrews was the worst example of our confusion. It had aped the worst excesses of Western life; strip joints, discos, even opium dens had sprung up during our exile and groups called the Footpath Boys roamed the streets, fighting and stealing. Those who said the President was communist and would nationalise everything could not have been more wrong. Emo surprised everyone with his attitude to capitalism. He promised social justice, education, work and asked for collaboration from everyone, including the capitalists who were needed to get the shattered economy on its feet. The police force was reorganised and soon Emo had cleaned up the major cities and towns. He fired any civil servant guilty of corruption and forced his ministers to take an oath saying that they would make no financial gain out of being in office. He began to be known as Emoti, The Incorruptible. Though some called him a puritan when he refused to allow television into our country. He did this, and still insists on it, because he wanted us to jump into the twentieth century on our own and not sit open-mouthed and indolent before images of other cultures. How he hated our laziness! Throughout the Pacific and Asia we were known for it. The long lunch breaks, late starting and early leaving from jobs was forbidden. Some argued that it was our natural disposition but Emo saw it as a bad habit of the lazy and as such, it could be changed. He led the way by working until late and rising early, so much so, that it was thought by the credulous that he never slept at all and sometimes this was used as an argument against his determination to make us work harder, 'But President Emoti is unnatural, unusual. He shouldn't use himself as an example.' These comments annoyed him but he kept pushing his people. 'I will push you or drag you into this modern era,' he often said, 'until you see hard work as an essential part of your lives and realise that with it our nation can produce miracles.'

The ideas that flowed from his mind during this time were like a waterfall. Power had liberated him. He saw a nation unformed and promised he could develop it. He would take this group of heterogeneous people and make them into an homogeneous whole. He gave government jobs to tribal groups who had never been given power before and he sent troops into the jungle to stamp out tribal warfare. I remind you, Mr Gecko, of all the good things he did because, in so doing, you will recognise how far we have come since then and how easy it is to forget those exhilarating, heady days, days when a husband and wife had never been happier.

Our love making was wonderful; power invigorated him. He would say the most tender things to me in bed and after making love would still have too much energy and so would talk to me until the small hours of how he was going to transform us: 'If we don't become a modern nation, then we will end up like those African states — worse off than they were as colonial backwaters and a parody of what they wanted to become after independence.' He was so full of the purpose of power in those early years that our childlessness did not bother him. 'Children will come when we are ready,' he said, when I was upset at being unable to conceive.

Everything he touched turned to gold — literally. A group of Japanese and American geologists discovered a golden mountain in the heart of the Night People's territory. Set in a forever rainy, misty jungle, the mountain's content of gold and copper was so high that it would soon, it was predicted by foreign experts, bring us a fortune in revenue. Foreign experts were brought in to exploit it. Emo's luck continued when a cure was found for the coffee and sugar cane fungus. Within two years the fungus had vanished. President Emoti was a hero.

Would that peasant with his pig's intestines have predicted such luck? Would his golden spleens cast across the parquet floor have told you that the perpetual rain would create such massive landslides and make conditions for mining so awful that it would take two years for the Golden Mountain to give us its riches. But when the money did come it allowed the President to do what he had been impatient to do. He had developed a grand scheme; he was going to import the best technicians and the best teachers to guide us into the modern world. We would, he promised us, become the equal of Japan and Singapore.

The West began to arrive and soon the port was clogged with ships bringing cars, computers, factory parts, tractors, engines, electrical equipment — anything, in fact, that could plug us into the twentieth century (except television — you were afraid of it because you realised how much your people would love it). Gold and copper prices rose and so we bought more and more. We were becoming a part of the Western world — consumed by the fire of consumerism. People flocked to the Port Andrews docks just to see the many ships anchored in the harbour waiting to be unloaded and their treasures paraded. Oh, what a time, dear Mr Gecko. Your bright, glowing eyes are like those of the eager spectators. The city was filled with all sorts of foreign technicians and experts (every foreigner is an expert went the rumour). New banks were opened, our first stock exchange was built, factories were designed and buildings started. Roads were tarred until they vanished into jungle tracks somewhere beyond the city. Parliament was in awe of this President. His vision was so extraordinary that it overwhelmed them. He was beyond tribal allegiances, beyond the small improvements most of them thought were major, and saw beyond the following planting season. He spoke in terms of decades and generations. No one had ever spoken of the future in that way before. We had always looked backwards, to the world of our ancestors who lived in distant dreamtimes. President Emoti did not speak of ancestors; he enthralled us with stories of future dreamtimes.

Down at the docks people gazed at the enormous wooden boxes and metal containers that were stacked on the piers and shouted out the President's name, praising him as a warrior and hero. Ever since the white man had colonised our country, and we had marvelled at their goods and envied their wealth, we had believed in cargo cults; the idea that Western goods would fall out of the sky like rain if only the magic invocation was right. But now it had happened! The magical wealth was arriving by sea from beyond the horizon. After years of waiting the people's patience had paid off. The President had clicked his fingers (or so the popular song went) and there, right before them, in the bellies of those huge boats and on the piers, were the goods for which they had hungered. Tribal sorcerers were exulted. After all the tribulations, disappointments and loss of faith in their powers, they had finally proved that they did have the necessary magic.

My hands are shaking. I am scared. Larenkeni had me taken out into the compound not so long ago. All the other prisoners were already lined up. Nambweapa'w escorted me to the front of the lines and placed me to one side as if I were on display. The suddenness of all this stunned me. I shivered with fear in the crisp night air. Prisoners were blinking because of the intense search lights that were shone onto us and some were yawning, not with tiredness but out of fear. I asked Nambweapa'w if I was going to die but he would not answer me. Looking at his anxious, young face, I thought I saw my answer. I felt him move away from me as if not wanting to associate with a dead woman. A figure approached out of the brilliant light. It was Larenkeni, closely followed by the governor. I cursed you at this moment. I wanted to shout out *Let the President kill me!* but my mouth was dry and my tongue felt like a piece of cardboard. Larenkeni smiled sarcastically at me and turned to the lines of exhausted, apprehensive prisoners. He motioned to an old guard, one of the few left in this world of youthful slaughterers, and indicated a prisoner at random in one of the lines. The old man plucked him out and stood him before Larenkeni who began to shout at him.

'What is your name?'

'Muala,' said the terrified man.

'Why are you in here?'

'I don't know.'

Larenkeni looked over at me. I was separated from the other prisoners so that the head of the Secret Police could make me look like his accomplice. He was going to make the other prisoners hate me even more.

'Of course you know. You have offended the President. Now confess what you did.'

The panic-stricken man confessed to all sorts of supposed crimes at Larenkeni's prompting. Finally, tiring of this spectacle, Larenkeni sent the man back into line. He then addressed everyone.

'See, if you confess, President Emoti is lenient. If you don't confess... well...'

He snapped his fingers and the old man was made to bring forward a young man from the coast. Handsome and with copper skin that was blotched with dark blue bruises from a recent interrogation, the young man stared defiantly at Larenkeni.

'This man here,' said Larenkeni, 'has done wrong and yet he has not confessed to it. Too proud, you see. And yet he is also stupid, too stupid to realise that President Emoti will forgive him if he confesses.'

He whispered into the old guard's ear. The guard was reluctant to do as he was ordered and the police chief had to gesture impatiently at him to get a move on. The old guard took out his revolver and placed it against the young man's skull. Just before the trigger was pressed the young

154

man looked at me, sneering. Unable to express his contempt for the President in person he used me as a substitute. I closed my eyes and heard the shot. When I opened them he was dead, lying on the ground, crumpled up like a sleeping child. Larenkeni caught my eye, he seemed almost victorious. I could not fail to get his message; I must confess or this would happen again and again until I was the victim. I turned away but found no solace in the eyes of the prisoners. They hated me even more. As far as they were concerned, the young man had died because, for reasons they could not fathom, I was stubbornly refusing to sign my confession. I was led through the lines of prisoners by Nambweapa'w and could hear their muttered curses *bitch, slut, cunt, dog shit* ... I stared into the search lights wanting their brilliance to dazzle me into oblivion.

I could not sleep when I got back to my cell even though I wanted to dream of you and, like an assassin, enter your bedroom and kill you. Scared and bewildered, I wondered if I should confess but gazing at your stony profile I knew that I was right not to. Once I confess you will have me murdered. As I pondered my future Nambweapa'w came into my cell. It was early in the morning and he was drunk and wild. He wanted to know where these pages were. He thrashed around the cell, throwing over the bed and hitting the wall to see if it contained my hiding place. When he came close to me I could smell the alcohol and spicy bark on his breath. Frightened of Larenkeni, he knew that if it were discovered that he had given me the materials to write my story then he was certain to die. He stood over me, 'I want to kill you,' he said quietly. As he stared at me I knew he was imagining doing such a thing. Unable to kill me he dragged me onto the floor and tore off my dress. I offered no resistance because if I did he would have throttled me; his eyes were ablaze with violence and lust. After fucking me he stayed inside me. I was too scared to move and, because he came from behind, I could not see what he was thinking. We stayed in this position until, after a time, I felt something moist and rubbery on my back. Gradually I realised that he was licking me, slowly, almost mechanically. For almost half an hour he did this, moving up my back until he reached my neck. As he licked my neck I felt tears and he whispered in my ear like a distraught child *you have bewitched me.* He pulled out of me and sat on the floor. I turned around and saw his exhausted and tear-stained face. He was a child in a terrifying world and was completely at a loss. I felt, indeed, that I had bewitched him. 'Where I came from we cut off the tits of witches and we burnt their cunts,' he said without emotion. He slowly got to his feet and left. I gazed at the dreamstone, it was still stone. The cell smelt of my spicy back. I touched the dreamstone, wanting it to crumble under my hand but it remained as solid as ever. Exhausted, I wept until I was calm. I remember when you cried, Emo; it was the last time you did — the day of the Pier celebrations.

Everything had led up to it. President Emoti was on the way to becoming a legend. He had ended the Time of the Fungus and he had found, somewhere in the dark interior, a Golden Mountain which was so huge that it could never be depleted. Ships from the West had arrived bearing gifts (we had been as awestruck as the Europeans must have been in the Middle Ages when the first ships arrived from the exotic East). The signs of change were becoming obvious. Western suits were more frequent, red betel juice no longer stained the footpaths as the use of it in the capital was forbidden, and we now called ourselves a nation rather than a country. People waited outside the palace or Parliament to glimpse their President and, if they were lucky (at this time everyone was lucky), he came among them, listening to their complaints. Like some benevolent god he would promise to fulfil their desires for a new dam in the Eastern provinces, for a road from one village to another, to free a woman accused of witchcraft, to install a telephone system for the hinterland — he even promised to try and help a man whose wife had gone missing in Port Andrews after being tempted by city life. Emo stood among these throngs like the calm eye of a hurricane; it was as if he found in their excitement the tranquillity of purpose. Every day, or so it seemed, the newspaper had a picture of the President. Look, there he is playing with computers which the Japanese have just installed at the airport ticket counter. There he is pressing the button to start the new electricity station so that at night the streets will light up as if they are in daylight. There's the model couple, President Emoti and his wife, Palu ('petite and beautiful' — my favourite description of myself), greeting the Prime Minister of Australia (who took credit for Emo's stay in Australia though, at the time, he refused to meet him because Emo was regarded as a revolutionary hot-head). Another picture of Mr and Mrs President touring the provinces in their jeep, while around them men and women in their face paint and arse grass dance with spears and clap wooden sticks of welcome. The President gives them a radio and they huddle around it believing they are listening to the voices of their ancestors. The President is full of conviction that these people will slowly come to realise that these are not the voices of the past but *your* voice and your voice is telling them that in the future no one will be illiterate.

The number of schools built in one year was a record, said the front page of the newspaper on the morning of

157

the celebration. It put Emo in a good mood as we ate breakfast. It is curious to think how light and airy the palace rooms were then. The servant from a coastal tribe joked in pidgin, a language which I was unable to master as well as Emo had (and that is another mark against me — proud Palu who won't speak a language she regards as being inferior to English). Shut that yodelling midget up! It is like the voice of a bat demon's slave. It is infecting the air. Someone turn down the radio! Miraculously someone does — even the guards dislike her voice. She thinks she is Queen but if Emo is ever overthrown she will be the first to be killed and her vocal cords will be slit with real hatred. *Tsk, tsk,* you say, but it's true, dear gecko.

It was decided we would walk down to the docks and so we trotted out of the palace, down the concrete steps and into a hot, summer's day. People lined the streets calling out 'Emoti, Emoti!' There were townsfolk and people from the Highlands wearing traditional clothes. They banged drums and yelled as if possessed by some euphoric fever. We were both surprised by the number of people lining the road to the harbour and by their excitement, forgetting just how important ceremonies and public displays of wealth are to our people. Even the besuited city workers, having been given the day off from work, laughed and shouted. A few people broke through the army and police cordon and touched the President on the elbow, a gesture which meant they thought him a magician and a chief. These people had come from the backblocks and had heard only the myths and legends about this new leader. Now he appeared before them, leading them to the beach where he would display the magnificent wares his magic had conjured up. Another time Emo would have shooed them away, annoyed at their superstitious touching, but this day he was above irritation. He was flying with the seagulls circling noisily above his head, which had ventured from the beach up to the palace as if to greet and escort him to the docks.

When we arrived there were so many people that we found it a difficult task to get through to the dais where Emo was to proudly unveil his vision of the future. With us on the dais were the ambassadors of those countries from whom we had bought most of what lay unopened on the docks. The noise was extraordinary. People yelled and laughed and the musicians from tribes all over the country played, trying to drown out the music of others. Beyond the milling crowd I could see, once I stood on my tiptoes, hundreds, if not thousands of wooden crates and metal containers. Knowing that such things as computers or electrical gear did not have the same immediate appeal, Emo had waited for this moment to astonish his people. In those boxes and containers were tractors, fridges, lawn mowers and behind those things were cars, covered in plastic sheets. In his speech the President told his people that these objects were the first of many and that we had entered a prosperous new world. The Highlanders, the noisiest of all the tribes, slapped their thighs and whistled in wonder at the vision President Emoti presented them. Their excitement was so infectious that I wanted to join them but I sat still, trying not to squirm, trying to be as calm and self-contained as my Emo or the ambassadors who marvelled at the enormous crowd and the way the President could quieten them — their short speeches had gone unheard in the general racket. When the signal was given, forty or so men, wearing special uniforms, ran towards the crates. The spectators standing behind the cyclone fence watched as the men pulled the covers from the gleaming cars. Unfortunately the hot sun had melted the plastic and patches of the covers stayed stuck to the car bodies, like peeling skin on burnt backs. The spectators didn't mind, however, and they cried out, 'Look! Look at the cars! See the colours! That's a tractor — look at them all!' And indeed, the dock did seem impossibly crowded with the vehicles. The throngs pushed against the fence, wanting to get a better look, even hoping to touch these magnificent objects. Emo was pleased; he was giving his people a glimpse of the future. The Australian ambassador leant forward and whispered in my ear, 'Your road statistics will soon resemble ours.'

I stood up to get a better look. Emo smiled as he sat contemplating the scene. He thought I was standing because I was short but I felt as if I were being invisibly tugged towards the crowd. Like a child I wanted Emo to lift me up in his arms and give me the best view, just as a father would hoist his daughter up onto his shoulders. Mr Gecko, there I am — a grown woman, and the President's wife, and I am still as excitable as a kid.

As I stood looking at the cars and tractors arranging themselves on the dock I tried not to yell out in my exhilaration. Emo joined me and when his arm brushed mine I sensed him jolt at my suppressed excitement. I want to tell him *Emo, I want to run up and down the pier, waving my arms and jump up and down and scream out with delight.* (Look, I can almost see myself weaving and ducking through the noisy crowd. Look! There goes Palu, minus dignity, minus self-control...)

'I didn't expect so many people.'

'No,' I said proudly.

'When I was in Australia I dreamt I could do something

like this. Something that would show the people in one moment — in one single moment — what we can do.'

The cars and tractors started up with a synchronised roar. The crowd roared back in response. The idea was that the cars and tractors would be driven through the main street of the capital to the football ground and there go on display with other, less impressive things like water pumps and chain saws. While the cars slowly and awkwardly positioned themselves on the narrow dock, the guards tried to clear the gates to allow them through. A tractor nearly collided with a car and, veering to avoid it, headed towards the edge of the pier. I can see that moment now, almost in slow motion — the stick figure twisting the steering wheel and the heavy back wheels not responding, the tractor perched on the edge, as if deciding whether to jump or not, and then tumbling over the side, the driver unable to scramble free. It vanished and a moment later a large wave of water landed on the pier. A silence came over us all, broken by a sudden smashing sound. Two drivers, their attention on the tractor, had crashed into one another. This started a chain reaction and twenty or so cars slammed into the rear of the one in front. Then a shout went up as the wet and bedraggled tractor driver appeared, pulling himself back onto the pier. He stood up and waved cheerfully to the crowd while the car drivers inspected the damage to their cars and yelled abuse at each other. The fence finally gave in and excited people tumbled forward, rushing to touch the cars and sit in the tractors.

I didn't know whether to laugh or cry. There was a growing anger beside me. Emo, shocked by what was happening, was grim-faced. The ambassadors were crowding the front of the dais, some of them smiling as if they were watching the antics of children.

'Let's go,' he said hoarsely. Coldly furious he grabbed my wrist with a vice-like grip.

'Emo, it was an accident.'

He paid no attention to my apology for his own people and nodded to the ambassadors who did not know how to respond, except for the Japanese ambassador who bowed deeply as if expressing the humiliation Emo felt.

We hurried towards the car that was supposed to have taken us back to the palace in a triumphant procession but the chauffeur had disappeared into the pandemonium. He was no doubt admiring the new model cars he wished to drive. I told Emo that I would drive us back but he was stubborn in his fury and said we would return the way we had arrived. As we walked out of the dockyards more excited people ran past us, heading towards the crowd which was spilling over the cars and tractors like ants devouring honey beetles. Angry and humiliated, Emo paid no attention to the people running past us. He retreated into himself and we walked in silence. I wanted to tell him that it didn't matter, that these sort of incidents happen in every society, but I knew he would not listen to me. His people had disappointed him. The road back to the palace was red with betel juice spittle and the sight only served to confirm for Emo his growing belief that his people were incapable of rising above their primitive state.

He refused to see anyone for the rest of the day. That night in bed, after I turned off the bedside lamp, I felt warm tears on my shoulders. He pressed himself into me in a desperate desire to lose himself in my body. 'They let me down, Palu. In front of everyone, they disgraced themselves and let me down.'

It was the last time he cried. He did not understand that

he was partly at fault. His actions had confirmed his people's beliefs in cargo cults and what they saw on the docks was not a vision of the future, but an act of magic. He had wanted them to see how wonderful these things were and how, through hard work and effort, these magnificent goods could be theirs. But there had been no time to teach the lesson of hard work and even if he had tried to drum it into his people in the way he wanted to, they would have told him how he had been lucky, and if it hadn't been for the magic of the Golden Mountain there would have only been a few miserable crates on the docks. Something in Emo died that day. He no longer trusted his own people; they had failed him.

'Palu, come out, you bitch. You witch! Come out, Mrs President!'

I heard this just as I was finishing the words above and then stones clattered against my wall. A pebble came in through the cell window, smashed against the far wall and dropped at my feet. I stood on my chair and looking out the window, saw a guard throwing pebbles at my wall, yelling abuse. It was the guard whom Larenkeni had forced to kill the young man. Demented by what he had done, he was taking out his frustrations on me. Some guards escorted him away. He turned back and saw me peering at him from my window. 'You caused this!' he screamed. I sat on my bed, sick to the stomach at how crazed the old man had become by his duty here. I wanted to throw you against the wall. Smash you into small pieces and throw your remains into the river. As if sensing my anguish Nambweapa'w appeared.

'*You* drove him crazy!'

163

'I didn't.'

'He said you made love to him in his dreams and got him to kill his own family.'

'That's not true. Look at me, I'm shaking like a leaf. Hold me.'

'If I hold you, you'll devour me. You've already bewitched me.'

I tried to explain that I hadn't, but Nambweapa'w, paying no attention to me, looked away at my gecko which gazed at him from near the crack where he hides. 'I hear you talking to this gecko. Only a witch can talk to lizards and geckoes.' He moved closer to me. I smelt alcohol on his breath. 'You are in my mind all the time. Ever since I first saw you when you arrived. That is the President's wife, said someone. You turned and looked at me, smiling with a witch's smile. You saw a victim when you saw me. I know about witches. Look at you, twice my age and yet I have done things for you I would never have done for another woman.' He leant over me, swaying slightly. 'I know where your power is. It's in your cunt and it's in your eyes.'

I saw that he wanted to tear me apart as simply and cleanly as ripping a piece of paper. He had come before me without eating spicy bark because he was testing his willpower.

There was the sudden sound of someone clearing his throat and Nambweapa'w spun around to see who else was in the cell. It was the gecko, eyes aflame, staring at us both. Nambweapa'w picked up the pebble the old guard had thrown into my cell and hurled it at him. The gecko was too quick for him and vanished into his hiding place. Mr Gecko, it was the worst thing you could have done at that moment because he thought I made you mock him. He saw it as the witch showing off her powers. He leant forward and said quietly, 'When you are executed, I'll do it. And you'll

164

die the way witches die. In agony and pain. You bewitched the President but I'll defeat you.'

After breakfast I was strangely sleepy and my limbs and mind became numb. I slept for some time, dreaming of you. Over and over again, like a dream in a fever, I saw you enter the palace reception room. Your presence was truly lifelike; you moved slowly, speaking slowly to assembled aides in a whisper (so they had to lean forward to catch your words as if catching precious drops of water in a desert) and your eyelids drooped as if already tired of their presence. They began to speak and a slightly bemused, unshakeable half smile appeared on your face. It was as if you were looking down from a great height on tiny insect creatures. After they had spoken you said nothing for a long time. Your art of silence has been perfected and the people, sensitive to the unusual, are awed. Your minions shuffled and looked uneasy. I thought I was already in the room but I saw myself enter and you shuddered to see me as if I were a ghost. You opened your mouth to speak but dark brown bile poured from it, down your white shirt and black suit. Standing there, covered in your own sickness, the minions did not know what to do. No one had ever touched the President. Someone went for a doctor and all the time your eyes were on me. As I stared back at you your body turned to stone and from a distant corridor your words began to seep into me:

'Everyone thinks he can turn his arse left or right but I will crush, crush it into flour and pass it through a sieve. I am a realist — if you are asking what I am. I can listen to very beautiful speeches, I can speak them but I remain doctrinaire and a realist which means I never permit myself to be intoxicated. I am equal to myself, in balance with myself. To be intoxicated is to be beside oneself. I am not beside myself. I am in a new phase of my political life. If I am,

165

then you are, then this country is. There is no change without gunfire. The nation must be under arms. The supreme chief must always be ready beside his soldiers to make respected what is respected which means you, which means me. Intoxicated people are not respected. Those who are intoxicated by the wind, by drink or stupid ideas will be treated like drunks. Remember this is not for my own good, it is for yours. I entered this struggle for *you*!' Your speeches are becoming more turgid, Emo. Words are being swallowed up by your darkness, too. What of the guards here, what are these simple youths to make of this theory of intoxication? Perhaps I have not listened closely enough to your voice recently but it is sounding tired, almost dispirited, as if even the energy of tyranny were vanishing. Perhaps I imagined the tremor in your voice, half believing that my dream had been real and you were beginning to grow exhausted from the sickness.

I look at your stone face and hear a squealing sow. A carving knife is thrust into its stomach. A slit is made and a hand plunges into its steaming insides. Its entrails are scattered across the floor. Can you see your future in the heart and intestines lying on the bloody floor?

Even though President Emoti was bitterly disappointed by the farce at the docks he did not entirely abandon his people. He had too much energy for that. Perversely, he ordered more and more goods as if by overwhelming his people they would eventually take all these new things for granted and would never become intoxicated by them again. When the price of gold and copper reached new heights so did the crates on the docks. You should have seen it, Mr Gecko, it was like a mountain. From the palace I could see beyond this mountain to the sea where more ships waited to unload.

The Parliament complained about this mania for development, saying it was too fast, too quick. Emo paid no attention to his critics as he had no time to lose.

But the mountain did not move. It grew larger and so did the number of ships in the harbour. Unable to unload they stayed for months growing rusty in the tropical sea. In his hurry to develop the nation Emo failed to understand just how unprepared we were for it. The mountain of crates and containers sat on the docks because the wharf workers had only a few forklifts to shift the enormous number of crates. There were not enough trucks to transport the goods to the places for which they were destined. The wharf became a centre of chaos. It was said that once, when the President ordered containers to be shifted from the docks because of the pressure of shipowners who wanted their ships unloaded, the wharf workers deliberately pushed them over the side of the pier into the deep harbour waters. Yet even a drastic action like this did not help clear the backlog. Machines rusted in the monsoonal rains and the rotting smell of corrupted food (hidden somewhere in mislabelled containers) filled the docks and wafted up the hill into the city itself. The foreigners complained about the delays. Computer and electrical systems could not be finished until all the parts had arrived — but where were they? On the bottom of the mountain, in containers wrongly marked school books, or out to sea on those sleeping ships? Emo had the wharf overseers and transport organisers brought before him, calling them incompetent and stupid, but it did no good. They shrugged and averted their eyes. Not wanting the President to see their gums and teeth stained with betel juice, they mumbled that someone else was to blame.

The mountain grew even more enormous in Emo's dreams and, unable to sleep, he often spent the night staring at

167

it from the western balcony. He had ordered night shifts to try and help clear the backlog and so the mountain would be feebly lit up by poor quality arc lights. The trouble was that even having a night shift did not seem to diminish the mountain for as soon as some crates went another ship arrived to unload even more. The narrow piers and antiquated equipment, which kept on breaking down, did not help either. What made Emo particularly frustrated was that from the eastern balcony he could see the half finished factories and buildings and knew that their development was stalled because it was taking months, even years, to get the necessary parts and equipment from the docks. Didn't these half finished buildings bother his subjects? They didn't, he reasoned, because there was no sense of urgency down there on the mountain. 'Look how slowly they are working,' he would say, staring at the distant figures moving lethargically in the frail light. 'It's as if they work in slow motion. I know they say I have a mania for development but they have a mania for laziness.'

'You're pushing them too hard,' I would respond, trying to get him to ease the pressure on himself and his own people, but he thought that if he relented, even slightly, the inertia of our nation would defeat him and that he, too, would be consumed by our lethargy. He hoped the people would be encouraged by seeing how the foreigners threw themselves into work and were not satisfied until a project was completed. Yet our people watched this seemingly frantic behaviour in astonishment, amazed at such effort being put into something that did not seem essential to their lives and that they had done without for thousands of years.

Although he did not speak about it I knew that Emo's hurt was growing deeper and was rooting itself in his personality. He sought out the company of the foreign experts and the ambassadors in the hope that their words and praise would make his vision seem possible. At dinners and parties the foreigners praised this black man who spoke in their own manner and who extolled their methods and visions. Afraid of his own people's incompetence (or what he saw as their incompetence) he found that these Westerners renewed his optimism. They loved the President and his wife. We were what our nation could become, the brilliant Mr and Mrs President prodding a tardy nation into a new era. The talk was of new projects, of literature and of super highways linking our impenetrable country. A few foreign critics thought that his mania for development was misplaced but he would say of these critics that they wanted our nation to remain backward because then they could continue to look down on us. You must realise, Mr Gecko, that these were heartfelt words. He hated the idea of us forever remaining a post-colonial backwater. He also realised that some nations wanted us that way. It is like those do-gooders who tell Australian Aborigines or South American Indians that they must remain true to what they were ten thousand years ago, so that they can be admired for being primitive. And what happens to these tribal people? They end up like rare animals in a zoo, gazed at, stared at, and oohed over, for being freakish and close to extinction. Emo feared we were in danger of becoming like those zoo animals and every time he saw tourists taking pictures of the backland people wandering awestruck through Port Andrews wearing only arse grass he would cringe. He also hated tourists buying tribal artefacts from street pedlars because those cheap wooden masks and carved alligators gave Western visitors the impression that those things were all we were capable of making. He could see those masks on American and Australian suburban walls and could hear the whites commenting *how pretty. Those primitives are good with their hands, aren't they?* Yes, it was a mania he had but it wasn't irrational. It had purpose. Forgotten now is the fact that President Emoti's exiling of artefact pedlars was not an act of folly.

And what of the mountain? It was huge and stayed that way. What is the myth now? Perhaps the new truth is that conspirators made certain that those crates would never be shifted from the docks. Incompetence became conspiratorial.

I sense your stony eyes staring at the entrails of the pig. Is there a meaning in that grey, smelly intestine curled across the floor like an ancient snake?

One night while we slept I became aware of a presence in our bedroom. I woke and saw a dark figure standing before our bed. For a moment I thought I was dreaming of the grass demon who had come to our college hut years before. I woke Emo and turned on the bedside lamp. The man jumped with fright. He was smothered in black oil and sprinkled with red dust, the signs of mourning for coastal tribes. 'How did you get in here?' Emo asked in pidgin and then in English, but still the young man didn't understand. Then, as he stared at the anxious, dumbstruck young face, Emo recognised the man as being a childhood playmate. He spoke to him in their own language and learnt that his father had died and that the tribe wanted him to become chief. Emo was placed in an awkward position; if the son of the chief doesn't assume his father's position then the tribe is considered to have 'broken the string'. Since becoming President, Emo had not seen his father for fear that it might weaken his resolve. His strength to govern his young nation had come out of a desire to forget his past. Yet for all his hatred of tribal life and its suffocating parochialism he felt a sense of guilt

170

at the thought of being responsible for breaking the string. The messenger and he went into the study and I could hear Emo's irritated voice and the quiet certainty of the young man. They talked on and on, Emo trying to convince the messenger that it was impossible for him to become chief. He took the wide-eyed young man on a tour of the palace, showing him how he had a duty to his country that was more important than any responsibilty to his own tribe. Haunted by the prospect of breaking the string, the messenger, although awed, could not see anything more important than the issue of the tribe's new chief. If the string broke then there would immediately fall on the whole tribe a time of terror and bloodshed as the young men fought for the chiefdom. It had happened before and the strife had all but decimated the tribe. During this period other tribes had invaded them, killed the young men and run off with their women.

The negotiation between the two men continued until after dawn when a decision was finally reached. Emo would nominate his first cousin as substitute for chief but he would remain the true chief in-absence. The compromise amused Emo who, when he told me, laughed, 'I'm chief but not chief. Isn't it wonderful how a tribal mind works?'

What is this terrible sensation of oppression I feel in my stomach? It is as though the fortune teller has his hand in my entrails and is ripping them out, preparing to cast them onto the floor. Mr Gecko, sing to me!

And he did sing to me and my stomach calmed. Are you causing this nausea in me? Did I detect your stony mouth smiling? You are incapable of laughing nowadays. If such a tribal messenger appeared before you now the first thing you would do is purge the guards for allowing someone to

171

sneak into the bedroom undetected. Then, of course, there was no threat of assassination and you did laugh at the incident. 'Here I am, President of the whole country about to become chief of my tribe. Everything in this place is topsy-turvy.' He viewed the whole thing as a joke and yet I suspected, as we were driven to the end of the coastal road two days later, that the real reason he was so light-hearted was because his father was dead. Occasionally he had mentioned how stern his father had been and I had gathered that he had been particularly aggressive towards his son. Emo had rebelled against this treatment by running off to the only mission school in the district and it was at this mission that he had the car stop.

The mission school was empty, the two classrooms run down and vandalised. Emo showed me his schoolroom and pointed to the wall where he had seen his first angel. 'I had heard of this place through my aunt. She said boys could learn to know a new type of magic here. The priest allowed me to stay in his house because I was frightened to return to my father after running away. When my father came to take me back Father Gibson stood up to him, telling my father that I would become a better chief if I knew about the world. And if I knew about the world then I would have stronger magic!' Emo smiled as he remembered Father Gibson's phrase 'stronger magic' and picked up a battered hymn book. He turned over its grubby pages, then dropped it back on the floor and gazed at the broken walls. 'The angels had more powerful magic than any of my father's demons. And, of course, after learning about the world who wants to return to living on a dirt floor. After the coffee plantation, did you want to return, Palu?' I shook my head and followed him outside to where members of his tribe were arriving to escort us to his village along the hill tracks. He paused in the unkempt garden, plucked a scarlet flower from a hibiscus tree and stuck it in my hair, his nervous fingers revealing how apprehensive he was about the ceremony that was to follow. Even though it was a gesture of love from a man who felt awkward making such gestures, I saw only an infinite hurt in his eyes. The lack of enthusiasm among his people for his modernisation, and its sullen pace, were creating a wound that would not heal and was, in fact, growing bigger.

Picture us, Mr Gecko: President Emoti is wearing his ice blue safari suit, Mrs President is in a white silk skirt and blouse and our four aides are in their smartest military uniforms. We are surrounded, as we wind our way through the narrow tracks, by the young men of the tribe, their bodies painted with white clay and, being temporarily leaderless (and therefore like women at the mercy of the moon every month), their penis gourds are splashed with blood.

The village was on top of a hill overlooking a valley on one side and the ocean on the other. From this position the tribe could see its many enemies. The women were tall and strong and the men handsome in the familiar coastal way of Emo. He was unsettled, though he pretended not to be and wore a half smile as if he were bemused by it all. But I could see the tenseness in his eyes (those eyes which are now impenetrable) and he fidgeted with the handkerchief in his trouser pocket. Emo had already warned me that the tribe disapproved of me because they thought I had stolen him and so I did not flinch when the women tried to humiliate me with their stares.

Emo's father had already been buried for five days but soon after we arrived he was taken from his shallow grave, his body partly digested by the earth. The smell of rotting death filled the village and penetrated our skin. Emo looked away as his crumbling father was shifted onto a litter of banana leaves. Then the mourning women wailed over their dead chief. Pretending to watch, Emo's eyes sought a spot above the women and stared into the jungle. Once their ritual mourning was completed, two elders guided Emo to the corpse. As they led him towards it Emo glanced at me as if seeking help. It was an expression that Emo had previously reserved only for his angels.

He was placed before his father and he stood staring at the decayed body for a long time. The tribe looked on, waiting for him to do what was required of him. He closed his eyes and, momentarily, I thought he was dropping off to sleep. Suddenly something coarse erupted from his throat as if some violent obstruction were being expelled and he bent over, spitting on the corpse; thereby sending part of his own soul into his dead father's so that both could remain united in death. Then, without much conviction, Emo mumbled the required formula for taking over his father's position. Standing before the decomposing body he seemed absurdly out of place in his Western suit, yet the incongruity did not bother the tribe. Their primary concern was to make sure the string was not broken. After completing the words Emo made as if to move away but he abruptly turned back, almost as if he had caught a movement of life in his father. Emo's distant, ironical expression changed. He grew transfixed by the corpse, staring at it for a long time, his silence making the elders of the tribe uneasy. I was wondering if he had been caught in some deathly magical spell when he suddenly startled everyone by screaming. He screamed three times in quick succession, the sounds erupting from him as if having escaped from a hidden prison of pain and exploding around us. Before we could recover he shouted out his father's name, yelling so loudly that it pierced the veil of the afterlife where his father's soul was heading. Then, as if he had been shot, Emo fell to his knees, prostrate before the ruined body, his face twisted in grief. I shuddered at the terrible power of it all. *Was this nightmarish behaviour really part of my beloved Emo?* He had always laughed at such traditions, calling them 'primitive' and 'basic', now it was as if his past had finally broken into his soul and taken root. He fell forward onto the corpse and lay there for some time, then rose to his feet looking confused as if only now recognising where he was and unable to remember what he had done. His eyes fell on me. Bewildered at his own behaviour he silently sought my explanation for it. In other circumstances he would have been embarrassed and angry at having been seen to behave in so public a manner but he was beyond feeling such emotions. Before he could collect his thoughts the elder tribesmen took hold of him and escorted him into his father's hut. The women sat me down in the centre of the village, making me face the corpse. Singing mourning songs they shifted the body from its litter of banana leaves and placed it in a shallow hole filled with hot rocks and there, throughout the morning and into the afternoon, it cooked.

Near evening Emo was led from the hut, helped by two men. His eyes were glazed as if he were drugged. He tried to smile as he passed me but the result was lopsided and stupid. He wore arse grass and a penis gourd, and his hair was plastered with clay and mixed with leaves and bird of paradise feathers. He was seated into the chief's chair, which was in the shape of an alligator standing on its hind legs with the seat extending from its belly. It had sharp, monstrous teeth and evil eyes. Emo mumbled for a cigarette and he was given one but his trembling hands could not hold it and it fell onto the ground. His glazed, distant eyes stared past me into the darkness that was possessing him. His fears about being swallowed up by his primitive past were coming true. His blood stopped flowing and his veins clogged with the ashes of his ancestors.

His father was dug up and cut into pieces which were then given to the villagers as relics to protect them from evil spirits. A small piece of his father's skin was fed to Emo and in eating it he absorbed the best qualities of his father. I found it difficult to watch him being engulfed by the very rituals he deplored, yet I felt it was not really Emo who sat under the shadow of the alligator's jaws but another man I had never seen before. The body that sat in the chief's chair was slack and hollow as if it were there merely as a sponge to soak up the superstitions and spirits of others.

As night fell all of the tribe's pigs were slaughtered and eaten. The village smelt of burnt pork. Men and women got drunk on cans of beers especially bought for the occasion and sang and danced, exhilarated now that they had been liberated from the fear of breaking the string. During these wild celebrations Emo had to sit in his chair, aloof from it all and so, as the night wore on, it seemed as though he were presiding over a binge that was his creation. Men deliberately cut their chests to test their manhood, couples ferociously rubbed their cheeks until their faces ran with blood and the older people ate until they vomited, then ate more. Unable to resist the fun Emo's four aides joined in the eating and drinking until they, too, fell to the ground senseless.

I awoke just before dawn. Emo was sitting in his alligator chair, his eyes wide open as if he had not closed them once during the night, and he was so still that he seemed to have almost become part of the chair. Then, as the dawn light filtered through the trees, his head began to move as if it were not part of his body, and it slowly surveyed the litter

176

of the night. People were asleep where they had fallen and the remains of pigs lay scattered on the dirt as if some giant animal had torn them apart. The smell of burnt blood, lust, sweat and dead human flesh hung in the air like a mist seeping into the very marrow of one's bones. Taking it all in his eyes passed over me as if I did not exist and then stopped to stare at the four soldiers sprawled on the ground. A slight smile appeared on his face. At the time I did not know whether it was a victorious smile at having presided over this chaos or a smile of relief at having survived it all. Now I would say that his smile was one of condescension; those four soldiers were too weak to keep themselves detached from such celebrations and their weakness was his strength.

Late in the morning, he gave his substitute the chief's spear, thereby handing over his authority, and we were escorted back to the car by the satisfied elders. Driving back to Port Andrews Emo was quiet and withdrawn. I wanted to know exactly what he had gone through inside himself but I knew he would never tell me as it was taboo for a woman to hear such things. He never made reference to the ceremony again but it *had* changed him. A sense of his past now became a part of him. He no longer talked disparagingly of 'primitives' and he began to refer to our past as something that must be incorporated into our culture. Rumours spread about the secret ceremony and it was said that he had been made the great chief of all chiefs and that he was none other, in fact, than Sido, the legendary warrior-hero who was known by different names throughout the country but who was believed by all to be going to return after thousands of years spent fighting demons in the underworld to become the greatest chief of all. Emo would have once laughed at these rumours but now he exploited them and when backblock people yelled out 'Sido' when they saw him, he waved as if to acknowledge himself to be the legendary hero. And as if to confirm his sense of continuation with the past, he began to accept the custom of purification, a ceremony he had always refused. When he visited a village a pig would be slaughtered for him and he would put his bare foot inside its belly, stirring its entrails and mashing its liver until he had become one with it and therefore one with the village. Like Sido he had to visit every tribe and become nominal leader of it. In accepting this dark world of myth and legends, Emo took a further step into the darkness of which he would eventually become Emperor. As each modern project stalled and he lost popularity with foreigners and members of Parliament, these visits to villages, as the unstated incarnation of Sido, restored his confidence; ironically, the very people he had once looked down upon became the backbone of his support.

Emo's resolve to revolutionise the nation did not so much falter as begin to lose its way. When one of the few projects was completed and it was pointed out that all the top positions had been taken by foreigners he did not seem to care, explaining that as foreigners knew how to work the new technology then they should run it. He had permanently lost faith in his own people and ever so gradually and insidiously we returned to being servants to a white elite, and it was they who had the largest houses, the most expensive cars.

The funeral had made Emo aware of his own mortality and a desire to have a child returned. Desperate, we tried everything, from Western ointments to the magical herbs of tribal midwives but nothing worked. Each month was a bloody disappointment. One night Emo came to bed drunk and he taunted me by calling me an 'immature coconut' that would never ripen. As if to mock my womb he sodomised me, biting me on the neck violently like some animal that

178

hates the very thing it lusts after. After he had cast me aside I yelled at him, telling him that it was not my fault we had no child and perhaps he was the infertile one. He shook his head and smiled mysteriously. 'You are the one who is infertile. You are the unnatural one.'

'How do you know?' I demanded. He said nothing but grabbed me, pushing me into the bed and straddling my body. A dark fire glowed in his eyes.

'Your cunt is a dead moon, Palu,' he whispered, and with that he leant over to the bedside table and sent the temperature graphs, thermometer and Polygala herbs scattering onto the carpet. He looked at me resentfully. I dared not move for fear of provoking him into violence. I knew he had heard the gossip that he was either impotent or infertile, and that he was not the true man a President was supposed to be. It was probably that night that he decided on a way to stop these rumours permanently.

This humid weather and Larenkeni's presence is affecting me badly. I feel nauseous and I am forever sleepy. I am trying to concentrate because I realise I may not have much more time but it is difficult. I dreamt I entered the palace. It was day outside, inside it was dark and my heart was full of dread. The palace was the dark lair it has become during the past few years. (The bright and airy corridors and rooms had become a labyrinth permanently darkened by the eclipse of Emo's spirit.) The corridors led to dead ends and false exits. I felt like a stranger in my own home. The guards, too scared to raise their voices, filled the maze with whispers like a breeze through the leaves of a dying tree. I found you standing before your mirror, staring at yourself as if hoping to catch your image doing something that you were not doing. Your face was pale with illness and your cheeks haggard. You turned on seeing me and struck me on the breast. I screamed out, but not with a human voice; it was the cry of a bird of paradise. The blow had turned me into a bird of paradise and I flew, wounded, to the chandelier. Feathers fell from my wings and breast and filled your mouth, smothering you. I woke as my featherless wings could no longer help me fly and I dropped to the floor.

For a moment I was bewildered and thought I was on the bedroom floor and that you had changed into a snake, and then I realised it was a real snake lying before me. It was small and plump and had a rat-like tail; a death adder. I wanted to cry out, yet I knew that because it was close any slight movement or cry would cause it to strike me. Scared shitless, I sensed someone looking at me through the door grating, but I dared not move my head to see who it was. I saw my Mr Gecko, on the wall behind the snake, crawling towards the safety of his crack. It would have been impossible for the snake to have come into my cell by itself, someone must have deliberately put it there. As I stared at it, willing it to slide away, I wondered if this were to be my execution. Unable to have me publicly executed Emo had decided, through his henchman, Larenkeni, to have my death seem an accident. I stayed frozen in my position, hunched up on the floor, for almost an hour, and I began to hallucinate that perhaps the adder was stuffed and it was a practical joke. As soon as I thought this, and, almost as if it realised what I was thinking, the snake began to move insidiously towards me. Paralysed with fright I closed my eyes as it neared me. I felt its body, like a sinuous muscle, sliding over my shoulder and around my neck where it stayed like a fleshy ruff for a few minutes and then slowly glided off me. I heard it drop onto the floor behind me and there was a long silence. Was it huddled up against my back or had it wound its way away from me? I had no way of knowing and I stayed in my uncomfortable position on the floor until I saw my gecko emerge from his refuge. I jumped to my feet and into the far corner. Then I turned back and saw the snake curled up on the head of my dreamstone.

It sat like a turban on Emo's head. The cell door opened and Nambweapa'w came in carrying a stick and a sack. He lifted the snake off the stone with the stick and placed it in the hessian sack.

'You tried to kill me,' I said, realising it was he who had put the snake in my cell.

'No I didn't. It must have crawled in here by accident. I looked in and saw you talking to it as it made love to you.'

'It did no such thing.'

There was no sense in saying anything more. He was triumphant. This had been his own private test and he was now certain that I was born of a snake and that I was a witch. He left with the snake triumphant.

Feeling light-headed I sat on the bed, my mind whirling with a thousand delirious images. When lunch came I could only eat a little and then threw up in my shit bucket. I began to feel better for having got rid of the badness that was inside me. Maybe the effort of trying to destroy you is, in turn, destroying me. I remember my father saying that a tribesman could not use the dreamstones all the time because the magic was too powerful and could destroy the dreamer. But I must continue. And I ask you — is there a weight on your head like a snake in the shape of a turban? Are you frantically trying to swipe it away? Or is all of this quite

181

pointless and are you perfectly healthy and contented in your darkness? I want to dream you to death but I am too bilious to sleep.

Larenkeni has returned to the capital, leaving the old guard who threw pebbles at my cell tied to a post in the compound. He is standing out there in a downpour, laughing. Sometimes he cries or whistles aimlessly. As I write these lines he is speaking to the ghosts whose presence he feels close to him, telling them he will not sleep, for if he sleeps he knows they will eat his liver, and without his liver he will have no afterlife. Larenkeni has left this mad old guard tied up in the compound to frighten the guards and prisoners into not relaxing after his departure. 'You will not eat my liver!' the guard cries out, then he laughs. My Mr Gecko has edged closer towards me as I lie on my bed writing. He is within touching distance of me, his heart beating quickly. He makes munching sounds as if warning me of some danger. I do not know what you are warning me about, Mr Gecko. I want to touch his heart, just to feel another heart that is alive, but I know my touch would scare him.

Your stony lips are smiling — what are you thinking about as you pace up and down the palace corridors waiting for Larenkeni to return with a signed confession?

Emo, I am going to hold on to your soul, like a tigress clinging to a bone, and I am not going to let go.

The shit bucket is getting more of my vomit as the day wears on. The guard is ranting endlessly. Those prisoners collecting rocks for the new cells yell at him to shut up but he is joyously confronting the ghosts who threaten to eat his liver. I feel empty but the vomit still comes. I sense you thinking about me, just as I always sensed you staring at me while I slept, your thoughts the treadmill of the same thought *why did I marry that immature coconut.*

*

I am pretending to sleep and I want you to touch me but we are an eternity away. Because I was denied access to your mind I read in your long silences everything terrible about our marriage, about me. I wanted to cry out *tell me what you're thinking!* I felt as though I were in limbo, waiting for your hand to reach out and pull me back onto the firm ground of reality. This state of suspension was part of your growing power over me. I made excuses for you; the difficulties of leading this country, the bad luck that was beginning to occur. It will pass, this turning away from me, I thought, then you will become the Emo I love, the one who people thought was a comet to which all other people were attached like cosmic debris. I recalled your strength, your excitement when discovering a new idea that made sense of the world, and your enthusiasm which carried me like a wind pushing a feather high into the sky. Now the bed is empty. More and more frequently the aides and flunkies do not allow me to see you of an afternoon and I hear a woman's laughter from your study — or am I imagining it, just as I imagine a sluttish figure vanishing down the rear steps of the palace? My thoughts of this period are made worse by my nausea and a song on the radio:

Won't you live on Golden Mountain
With the miners and the golden boys
You can't be sad on Golden Mountain
There's too much gold, too many toys.
On Golden Mountain
I picked up a rock of gold
Boy, it sure felt cold
Boy, o, boy, it sure got hot
Boy, it sure got hot.

She has never been to the Golden Mountain. I went once. As usual it was raining there. We flew in by helicopter because the road was washed out again. A giant red scar had been carved out of the top of the green mountain. The miners lived in a world of perpetual rain and mud. Emo and I had come to give the miners encouragement. Because of the rain and problems of transportation the gold was becoming more and more expensive to mine. The workers felt as though they were in hell and the foreign overseers could survive only a few months there. But as the price of copper and gold fell it was important that production be raised. Besides coffee it was our only true source of international income. As we toured the mine I talked to an American mining expert who had been there for three months. He had a defeated look about him and while we sheltered under his umbrella, he pointed to the distant valley. 'The people there think that this mountain is the home of bad spirits and that we are waking them up. I'm beginning to agree with them,' he said, interrupting himself as he grabbed me by the elbow to stop me slipping.

President Emoti's visit did not help production and a few months later there came reports of a bad accident. Tonnes of cyanide, used in processing the gold, had washed into the river which became clogged with dead fish and, soon, people, who had either swum in the river or drunk its water, were seen bloated and dead, floating down to the sea. The miners fled, fearing retribution from the local tribes. It was over a year before production was resumed but by that time the area was known as The Golden Death and it was said that the evil spirits had broken out of the mountain and were running berserk. Some even say that it was these evil spirits who captured the President's soul. Soon after gold mining production was resumed the prices of gold and copper fell again, and modernisation of the nation stalled even more. Projects stagnated, buildings remained unfinished and permanently hidden behind the steel cobwebs of scaffolding. Cars ceased to run for lack of parts and the electrical system, designed to depend on the uncompleted network of hydro-electric schemes in the Highlands, often malfunctioned. There was nothing Emo could do and it was said that his mania for development had consumed him, like fire destroying the very wood that gives it life.

A small bedroom in the palace became taboo to everyone, including myself. Initially I thought that Emo might be using it to meet his women but one afternoon I saw a wooden crate being placed outside the door. I realised, then, that he was seeking the comfort of angels again. A great fear was possessing him. One night at dinner with Colonel Akwanaamae and his wife, Emo and the Colonel talked about plots and informers. I pretended interest in Mrs Akwanaamae's talk about her attempt to learn French, but all the time my ears were focused on the men's talk of a coup and the suspicion that its leaders were several cabinet ministers. After the dinner guests had gone I ventured outside onto the balcony which overlooked the docks. Emo was watching the men pushing containers and crates into the sea.

'Why are they doing that?'

'Because they need space for the coffee.' It's the only thing that's earning us money at the moment. Havana has its cigar, India its tea, we have coffee,' he said sarcastically, seeing before his own eyes our return to being dependent on that hated colonial crop. Even this extreme action of the wharf labourers did not seem to make the mountain any smaller. It had been growing larger for a long time because few people wanted to take delivery of goods which they could now ill afford. Among the entrepreneurs, foreigners and the small

185

middle class, President Emoti had become a much disliked man.

'What they don't seem to understand is that I can do nothing. No one can. Until gold and copper prices rise we can do nothing.'

'Is that why people are plotting against you?'

'Yes.'

'If you feel there is nothing you can do, why don't you resign?'

He turned to me, his face condescending in the moonlight. 'You don't understand, Palu. I will win out in the end. I don't give up. That mountain down there will shift. Gold and copper prices will go up and the country will be transformed. You shouldn't doubt me.'

'I don't doubt you.'

'I am the only one who can keep this country together. Remember when we were teachers how I kept my classes interested and well behaved while your classes were always in chaos?'

I didn't know how to answer him. A hardness and distance had entered him. Like many leaders he found it impossible to willingly give up power. I went to bed and he vanished into the angel room, my words seeming to have decided him on something. Early in the morning I heard police sirens and gunshots in the streets. I asked palace aides what was happening but no one seemed to know. Late in the morning, after the gunshots had ceased, Colonel Akwanaamae arrived. I saw him hurrying along the corridor towards Emo's study, a triumphant smile on his face. Those who had planned the coup had been rounded up and jailed. Those who had tried to flee had been shot. I was not to discover until a few days later that most of the plotters were members of coastal tribes and part of their reason for wanting to over-

186

throw Emo was his willingness to give positions of power to the Night People. No longer able to trust his own tribal kind, Emo knew he could trust the pitch black skins as they were grateful to him for giving them power. In embracing the protection of Night People Emo had stepped further into that darkness that was becoming part of his soul.

Trusting no one and wanting no one to disagree with him, he retreated further into his own world. He began to play, not on the hopes and enthusiasms of his people, but on their fears. In speeches he talked of ghosts, spirits and demons as if he, like Sido, had personal control over them. The future was stagnant but the past gave him power over his people. Colonel Akwanaamae and his black demons grew stronger, threatening anyone who criticised the government. There were rumours that brutality and torture were becoming an epidemic. Larenkeni strengthened his secret police by employing Footpath Boys who took pleasure in tormenting citizens they did not like. Emo seldom came to our bed, preferring to stay up all night as if the darkness gave him strength. People saw his study light on in the early hours and the myth grew stronger that he never slept. As his authority became more dictatorial so his sexual drive grew less, as if the ambition to gain more power consumed everything else in him. He once said that when he had complete power then he would be able to modernise the nation without being held back by critics and narrowminded people, but the more power he had, the less the future interested him. It was as if he were becoming a piece of stone like my dreamhead.

As he changed from Emo into President Emoti I did nothing. I felt that as a carrier of a dead womb I was not entitled to say anything that might have awoken him to the changes in his personality. I was also in awe of his

187

relentless pursuit of power and, if the truth be known, I was frightened into submission by these changes in him. It was as if the bat demon had taken over him. As his speeches grew longer and more turgid, his conversations with me grew less. To find out his true state of mind I stole the key to his angel room and found it filled with dozens of stone, marble and plastic angels, most of whose feet or gowns were covered in fine sprays of blood. It was a room full of his fear. The angels stood before me petrified, their stiff wings paralysed and useless.

My wings are useless too. I am stuck here unable to fly away. Feeling ill this evening I lay on my bed unable to sleep. As I lay there, thinking of you, I noticed an unearthly glowing light slowly moving down the corridor. I heard men yelling out and Nambweapa'w burst into my cell.

'Come on, get rid of them!'

'Get rid of what?'

He grabbed me by the arm and hurried me out into the corridor. At the end of it was a swirling whirlwind of lights the size of pinheads. I heard noises behind me and saw two other guards also alarmed at the sight. The whirlwind began to move back down the corridor.

'You caused them. Get rid of them!' Nambweapa'w shouted at me.

Unsteady because of my illness, and unable to think clearly, I had no idea what this strange source of light was. The governor and his aide arrived.

'What is it?' the governor asked Nambweapa'w.

'Fireflies, sir.'

Now I understood why the guards looked so anxious; fireflies are a bad omen and mean someone is soon to die.

'How did they did get in here?'

Nambweapa'w pointed at me. 'She brought them in, sir.'

'Get her back to her cell.'

'Only she can get rid of them, sir.'

The men thought that because I was a witch I had made the creatures magically appear in the corridor. They saw the fireflies as being a bad omen for them but I saw in those whirling pins of light my own death in the near future. The guards prodded me to take control of that brilliant wind of light. I walked into it. The fireflies glowed and flew around me like thousands of tiny stars. I ordered Nambweapa'w to open the far door, realising they wanted to escape from this man-made cave. I waved them towards the doorway and they flew out into the night air. The guards and prisoners no longer need proof that I am a witch. They have seen me as a messenger of death right before their very eyes.

'Don't you understand, it was a coincidence that they appeared. I didn't cause them,' I said to Nambweapa'w after he took me back to my cell.

'There are no coincidences in life, Mrs President. Everything has a meaning.'

He looked tired and exhausted as if he had not slept for days. The fireflies were just one further confirmation of my being a witch. I was too tired to argue.

'I'm ill. Can you get the doctor.'

'He's not here.'

'Some headache tablets then?'

It was as if he didn't hear me because he turned on his heel and left my cell. I heard shouting and looked out into the compound. The fireflies were spinning around the old guard tied to the post. He was yelling at them to leave him alone for he feared that they foretold his death. Tomorrow morning he will be dead.

With all the concentration I could muster I dreamt of

you. Your eyes have changed, they are red as if you are incapable of sleep. Your hair is growing white. I saw you kneeling before the angels. You wanted to go to bed and sweat out the illness that is possessing you but fear kept you in their presence. I know what you want to do. You want to conquer your fear of me by giving Larenkeni permission to have me executed. Incapable of making the decision you left the angel room. Aides silently drifted out of the way of the ghost who walks. You have finally become the Phantom. Jayne talks to you but you do not hear her. A bat can only hear high-pitched sounds and everyone is talking too low for you. In bed you are wide awake. I am sitting on the bottom of the bed watching you as you watch me. Remember when we were in love an eternity ago? Your palace has become a cave and the darkness is turning you pale. You want to strangle me with your tongue but you lack the energy. We sit in the bedroom for eons, husband and wife, together in sickness. You want me dead, I want you dead, but we don't have enough energy to kill one another. I will take you with me when I die. I look to the ceiling, clouds of yellow, crimson, blue and green bird of paradise feathers fall on me.

Is this dream true? I want to be inside your mind, my illness infecting you.

I wish the birds of paradise would forgive me.

Three wishes. That is what one of the fairy tales Mister Bacon gave me to read said. Only three wishes; no more.

Mister Bacon, I am standing on your overgrown grave by the river and behind me I can hear the coffee bean fruit, the size of apples, exploding with ripeness and I am talking to you, asking for advice.

This page has become soaking wet with the sweat dripping

down my arm onto my fingers, until the pencil is too slippery to hold.

How long have I slept? I remember the tortuous effort it took to hide these pages and my crawling back to bed. My insides seem to have been eaten away. Is some demon inside me devouring my liver? My diarrhoea is worse and flies swirl around my shit bucket. Mr Gecko is growing fat. He waits like part of the wall and then, when one fly comes to rest, his tongue leaps out and he pulls in his prey. At least one of us is well, Mr Gecko.

I am trying to concentrate but I don't have much energy. I have been lying on my bed thinking of you and every time I do your voice comes on the radio. The voice sounds exhausted and it makes your speeches sound even more tedious. That beautiful, logical mind is no more:

'I am what I have always been, a man from the people who took power because you wanted me to. Took it forever. Never will he leave this palace which is so loved. President Emoti. I am already an immaterial being. I will not hesitate, as I have always said, to make red night for the triumph of my cause.'

And so it goes on and on and then Jayne's voice cuts the air:

> President Emoti
> President Emoti
> He is the father of us all
> He hears when you call.
> President Emoti
> President Emoti.

Delirious with sickness I yelled out, above the hideous noise of her song, 'Ripperty Kye A-hoo! Ripperty Kye A-hoo!' Nambweapa'w rushed in, wanting to hit me. 'How dare you make fun of her song!'

Unable to hit me he turned on my gecko who, too plump to move as quickly as usual, was slow to escape and Nambweapa'w smashed his tail against the wall. The tail fell off and the gecko scurried into his crack. I laughed at the manner of escape and Nambweapa'w turned on me, grabbing my arm as if he wanted to squash it like he had the gecko's tail. His roughness jolted me and I vomited on him. He grimaced and let go, his arm and shirt covered in yellow bile. I heard the sound of whistling coming from outside. There will be more killings soon. I smiled at Nambweapa'w's discomfort.

'Why don't you die!'

'I can't,' I said, swaying with sickness, trying to sound triumphant. 'I'm a witch — remember!'

He left the cell and a few moments later I heard that dreadful voice turned up as loud as the radio could go. Her voice pierced my ears. I shouted out 'Ripperty Kye A-hoo!' until I was too exhausted to do anything but croak. I slumped on my bed. I stared you you, wanting to bleed over you, pollute your very being.

When my stomach is empty I feel better, though I will try and eat something tonight as I need my strength. I don't know how many days I have been delirious with illness but I swear that your tail is starting to grow back, Mr Gecko. Yes, I know why you're glum; you're no longer as handsome as you were. I have always forgiven handsome people, just as I would forgive Emo's behaviour because at night when I lay next to his glorious body I could not imagine it doing anything cruel. If you were ugly Nambweapa'w I would never forgive your behaviour. One night at dinner, during the early days of Emo's Presidency, I remarked on the beauty of coastal men compared to Australian men I had seen, and the Australian ambassador said, 'Are you sure you don't have any Greek blood, Palu? Down through the ages they have always been susceptible to human beauty. The Byzantine historian, Anna Comnena, forgave the Crusaders everything if they were handsome.'

'Is it a weakness or a strength?'

'I don't know,' he smiled diplomatically.

'The Highlanders are well known in our country for their attraction to beauty. They place greater store by it than other tribes,' Emo said and went on to talk of how, when he had first been in the Highlands, he had seen Highlanders wearing seashells as if they were diamonds when any coastal person knew they were beach trash. There was a tone of condescension in his voice, though at the time, I took little notice, believing he was teasing me. For all Emo's talk of a united people he too, found it increasingly easy to categorise people according to their tribes, just as tribal people always gave primary allegiance to their own tribe, rather than to the nation as a whole. In many ways it did not surprise me when I heard reports that some Highland members of Parliament were plotting to overthrow the government because they were dissatisfied with the little Emo had done for them. Why was the cargo they had been promised still lying on the docks? Why had not the Highlands seen any of it? What about the roads and the electricity? They called themselves the forgotten people. Was it really true that the Highland members were plotting against the President? I have no way of knowing. Colonel Akwanaamae and Larenkeni gave Emo plenty of evidence but they were both Night People and both had a reputation for fabricating such evidence. After hearing of the plot Emo promised a 'Himalaya of corpses'.

He did not act for a week but then one morning he vanished into his angel room and not long afterwards I heard gunshots. I thought my ears were deceiving me; surely the gunfire wasn't coming from inside Parliament House itself? Not realising what I was doing, I rushed outside and ran down the road towards the Parliament. There were soldiers everywhere and they yelled at me, telling me that the situation was too dangerous. I paid no attention and ran on, not wanting to believe that such a barbaric act was happening in the very place of government itself. When I arrived the fighting was over. A Highlander was lying on the steps, his head blown off. A Night Man member of parliament dipped his handkerchief into the splatterings of brains and ran down the steps into the street crying out, 'Look! Look at the damn brains of a plotter!' Soldiers were carrying out the bodies of other slain members of parliament. Horrified by the obscenity of what had happened I ran back to the palace and banged on the door of the angel room. Emo opened it, exhausted. 'They have slaughtered men inside Parliament House itself, Emo!' He nodded as if he knew. The groin region of his trousers was stained with blood and glancing inside the room I saw a bloodied razor blade at the feet of a marble angel.

'It had to be done, Palu. They were going to try and overthrow me today.'

'What's happening is nothing more than tribal warfare! Parliament has been desecrated, Emo.'

He stared at me as if he wanted to crush me. 'You know nothing!' he said coldly and went back into his room of angels.

Larenkeni had all the wounded placed on the footpaths as an example to other would-be plotters. Guarded by policemen and soldiers the conspirators were left unattended, flies and insects drinking from their wounds. Highlanders who lived in Port Andrews cowered inside their homes, expecting to be arrested for complicity — as some of them were. Outraged by the slaughter a delegation of foreign ambassadors asked for an audience with the President. They were forced to sit in the waiting room for two hours beyond the appointed time. While he kept them waiting Emo sat in his chair, immersed in his own thoughts. I sat nearby like the good and loyal wife I was supposed to be and Colonel Akwanaamae and Larenkeni whispered to each other. Emo looked like a statue, devoid of life. It was as if he were a changeling. That is not the real Emo sitting there, I thought to myself, that is an imposter. When he eventually permitted the ambassadors to enter he nodded to each as though giving a personal greeting but, really, he was quietly cursing them in his own language. Unable to shout at them because he did not want to stop the flow of foreign money into the country, he sat silently and listened while the ambassadors complained about the 'act of barbarism'. Emo's silence and stillness were unnerving, even to me. When one of the ambassadors spoke about the slaughter being a vendetta against the Highland people, Emo turned to me. 'I am married to a Highlander — is she to die too? I have no grudge against Highlanders, only against conspirators.'

Mr Gecko, you ask why I didn't speak up and say *I believe that my husband may not have a vendetta against Highland people but Larenkeni and Colonel Akwanaamae do.* Maybe I could have stopped what was to come. Those prisoners who jeer at me and curse me in their sleep are right. I should have done something then. Yet, in my own defence, I wonder if I could have done or said anything that would have changed the course of events. My husband was impossible to communicate with. He was disappearing from me, vanishing like a ghost in the sunlight. He seldom slept with me and if he did, and we made love, he always sodomised me as if he were saying *this is what should be done to women with dead cunts!* I tried love potions and new dresses to win back his love but as he became more inhuman, so an emotion like love became abnormal to him. He perfected the monologue of silence. If I tried to talk to him he listened but did not reply.

He did the same with his cabinet or citizens who came to petition him. If they wanted a clue as to his thoughts he would smile his mysterious half smile which meant nothing and everything. If he did speak, he spoke softly and one had to lean forward to catch what he was saying. Everyone got caught up in the mystery of his meaning and his being. He was like a dust devil which sucks everything up into itself. His speeches grew illogical and where before he had spoken of the future in wondrous terms he now seldom spoke of it at all. His vision of the future had dried up, like a piece of skin curling up and shrivelling in the sun. The word 'President' began to take on greater meaning and he referred to himself in the third person as 'President Emoti'. In order to play his role as President Emoti he became a performer. When he spoke in Parliament, which was infrequent, he developed a curious persona. His voice deepened, his brow grew imperious and he flashed what he assumed to be a winning smile but which appeared to the listener as one full of menace. Sometimes I saw him walking down the corridors of the palace, when he thought no one was watching, and he would practise his gestures; stiffly flinging out his arms to indicate that he was emotional about a topic or walking with an almost supernaturally slow gait that unsettled people for its resemblance to a sorceror stalking his victim.

The natural for him became the unnatural and for his people, this artificial creation which was President Emoti

196

made him seem even more powerful. He became in their eyes a hybrid of Sido, the mysterious warrior-chief, and the cartoon character Phantom, the comic which had become the most popular in the country (it is Nambweapa'w's favourite also). Another leader's popularity would suffer if he seldom appeared to his people but Emo's absence from his own citizens made him seem even more mysterious and therefore powerful. The legend of President Emoti as an incarnation of Sido and the Phantom grew, and just as the Phantom lived in his cave, so President Emoti lived in his labyrinth of a palace. And what of his deformed fingers? A rumour spread that the legendary Sido had two deformed fingers. I grew angry at this sort of misuse of the people's credulity but could do nothing; the legend was becoming fact.

Emo played on the primitive past of his people such that primitive customs and beliefs became revolutionary values. 'Celebrate your tribal customs' is a saying that bores everyone now. His return to *authenticity* (another term that has become a cliche) was because there was nowhere else for him to go and also because he could use the darkness and fears of tribal customs and legends to keep power. Like a leader of ancient times, he saw himself as incorporating the nation itself. If the nation was well, he once said, then he was well and if he was sick then the nation was also sick. Who can argue with that now? Like the iris of the eye that opens wider at night so it can let in more light to see, so his soul opened to let in more darkness. In his own language opponent meant enemy and criticism was another word for conspiracy. He did not understand that his celebration of tribal values had created a new art form; stone age-modern. The tribal warrior drives to the place of pig sacrifice in a Western car. The spear is celebrated but it is the gun which is used. Tribal community life versus modern individualism.

197

Stone age and modern values were caught up in each other's fatal orbit, like boxers tied to one another, fighting to the death. At the bottom of all Emo's beliefs was the awareness that his own people had proved themselves incapable of becoming part of the modern world. A man becomes a despot when he no longer has faith in his own people. And Emo believes in no one and nothing. If only the people could understand your true hatred of them then they would destroy you! The only ideology you have is that of fear. I will make you truly understand fear. Look, even as I write your dream-stone is trembling and I know you are in the angel room cutting into your erect cock to give yourself courage. You realise, as you debate with yourself about my execution, that I am the last thing you have to get rid of, yet to get rid of me will excise your last links with anything you once believed in. I sense something else, too: *your fear of my power!* You clasp your bleeding cock believing I have infected you. Everytime you think about me, your illness gets worse. I am struggling with you in my waking dream and I have my white, furry tongue down your throat and I am infecting your liver. I am like a ghost salivating for it. You're struggling like a fish on a hook but I have to pull my tongue out because she is singing again and I cannot concentrate on destroying you. She is singing often these past few days. Her voice torments me. Emo, I detect your hand behind this. The radio at the end of the corridor is always on high volume now and she never stops singing. You are making sure I do not forget that *thing*, that tuneless creature who finally separated us.

Because I had taken all his semen and given nothing in return he called me a witch. 'You have castrated me, Palu,' he said, when he found that he was incapable of even sodomising me. I knew he occasionally saw other women but did he make love to them? Perhaps their newness helped his potency. I don't think it was the sex that interested him, it was more the desire to impregnate them — these silly girls that Luku-labuta, his favourite aide, found for him in bars or brothels. Colonel Akwanaamae's potency was an irritating reminder to Emo of his own failure. The colonel's wife had had six children in the first five years of marriage and the colonel often bragged that every one of his four mistresses had been impregnated. What a contrast to President Emoti who was supposed to be the great warrior-hero Sido who had fathered one hundred children before disappearing into the under-world. It was said that Lukulabuta sometimes journeyed into the backblocks to find tribal remedies for infertility and impotence. It was also said that he paid the girls he procured for the President handsomely to say that President Emoti was a great lover, and, if any of the girls became pregnant (no matter who to) he started the rumour that the President had caused her stomach to swell.

Yet that was not enough for Emo. One day I heard from a palace cleaner (aides and cleaners were becoming my only connection with reality as Emo hated me to venture outside the palace — he wanted me to stay in his darkness) that Lukulabuta had flown to Australia. This seemed a curious, even absurd thing for him to do, yet the details gave the rumour a great validity. It was said that a plane had flown out of the Port Andrews airport during a tropical rainstorm and it had had only one passenger. An airport worker had seen a face staring out of the rainy window as the plane taxied before take-off. The passenger was said to be Luku-labuta, whose face was impossible to mistake because of the ugly scars dug into its black flesh and the wide, popping eyes that gave it a forever astonished expression. Lukulabuta had been gone a week when Emo came to my room. I had been crying at my estrangement from him and thought my prayers had been answered when he appeared.

'Mr Andrews is dead,' he said simply.

I was momentarily confused as to who he was talking about.

'He died in a car accident a few days ago. I thought you might want to know.'

With those words he left my bedroom to wander the corridors like the ghost he had become. Over the next few days he grew edgy. The most discomforting facet of his nature had always been his ability to hide his moods but now his testiness was obvious and he yelled at his staff for the slightest misdemeanour. I began to realise that something important hinged on Lukulabuta's trip to Australia.

Six weeks later Lukulabuta returned. With him was someone Emo had been secretly seeking for years. He told me who it was as we were being driven to the airport. He told me of his affair with Louise and how she and Ted had separated because she was going to have Emo's baby. Louise had died soon after the child was born and the child had been placed in a series of foster homes and so it had been difficult to trace. I was so stunned that I could say nothing. He gave no thought to the brutality of what he was saying. So concerned was he to prove his potency (and look at his excitement as he sits beside me in the car — I have not seen him so animated in years) that he did not care that I would be publicly humiliated by his acknowledging the offspring of an illicit affair. I felt as though I were on the way to my place of execution. Once people saw that President Emoti was potent then I would be the one to blame. The dead moon of my cunt would be ridiculed by all. There is nothing more useless than a woman with a stone cold womb.

I began to cry. He looked at me, a puzzled frown on his face. I could see what he was thinking *why is this woman spoiling my great moment* ? He turned away to look at the approaching airport, obliterating my presence from his mind.

Lukulabuta came down the steps of the plane accompanied by a thin, black-haired girl carrying a cassette player. As they crossed the steaming tarmac I saw that she was about ten years old. I saw nothing in her face that resembled either Emo or Louise. On the contrary, her olive skin seemed more Italian or Greek. She shook Emo's hand nervously, saying hello in a broad Australian accent.

'Hello, Jayne,' said Emo stiffly, shaking her hand as if she were a visiting dignitary. 'This is Palu,' he added, motioning to me. She shook my hand and stared at me intently. There was something cunning about her young face as if she had lived her short life on her wits and was searching for any weaknesses she could exploit. She turned away from me and looked around apprehensively, never having seen so many black faces in her life. Emo escorted her to the car, chatting quietly. Lukulabuta was worried and jumpy, and he surreptitiously listened in on the conversation between his President and the child. It occurred to me that Lukulabuta might be duping him and that Jayne was in no way related to Louise or Emo. The more I searched that young girl's face for familiar traits the less I could find. In explaining how he had found her, Lukulabuta told of his arduous search of dozens of foster homes and orphanages, and then his miraculous discovery of her in Adelaide. With Louise and Ted dead it was nigh on impossible to check the story and, anyway, it wouldn't have mattered because Emo would never believe she wasn't the product of his loins. He needed her too much to doubt her. When he showed her off in public I didn't feel the humiliation I thought I would have. I had become convinced that she was a fraud and saw Emo's faith in her being his progeny as a sign of his increasing instability. How ignorant I was! I did not understand the full ramifications of this she-devil. I knew little about the legend of the warrior-chief Sido and so I did not realise that an essential part of the myth is that when Sido returns from the underworld to unite all the tribes that split when he departed on his journey to kill the Night demons, he conceives a white child with a white woman. Jayne was proof that President Emoti had, indeed, made love with a white woman.

For the first time in years Emo toured the backblocks, taking Jayne with him. He did not have to mention that he was the incarnation of Sido. The white waif at his side proved it. The more essential she became to his rule, the more we grew apart.

I hear birds of paradise! It is a curious thing but as I write I can hear the distant calls of birds of paradise. Listening closely I can tell that the calls are those of the male's cry for the female — the mating season is beginning. Am I dreaming this? They must be in the trees at the edge of the jungle. It is the first sign of jungle life I have heard since I have been in here. Strange to think that they are so close. Their calls carry easily from the jungle, a kilometre away, over the barren earth to here. I wish I could hear your voices more distinctly. Are you attempting to forgive me? Will I wake, dear birds, to find that my cell is covered in your feathers of forgiveness?

Getting out of bed I hold myself up and peer out through my window, half hoping I will see the birds dancing for me in the compound. The compound is empty except for the corpse of the old guard, still tied to the post. I try to listen, to understand more of what the birds are saying, but the radio is switched on and her voice drowns out my birds. Her awful taste in music has remained the same ever since her arrival. She brought with her tapes of Australian country and western singers and the palace corridors were soon filled with the loud drones of Slim Dusty, Big Mal and the Murrumbidgee Kid. Bored by this alien country, she bought a guitar and began to compose her own tuneless dirges. Emo thought she was talented and had her sing them on the radio. Her songs about true love and being a lonesome cowgirl in the jungle reached into the furthest corner of the nation, until her influence was so enormous that it seemed that every teenager was learning guitar and singing mournful country and western songs. I thought it hilarious at first but after a time it grew hard to laugh at her devastating influence on our music. She is never off the radio, even as I write she is yodelling one of her most popular songs:

> Tell me I'm your sweetheart
> Tell me we'll never part
> Our true love goes on and on
> My love for you is a song.

Dear old guard rotting in the sun, your liver devoured by ghosts, is your soul dancing to this music?

Jayne took Emo from me. We were drifting apart before she came but she completed the separation. Knowing I was suspicious of her she ridiculed my shortness, calling me a dwarf and when she was with Emo, and I was in their presence, she would call him 'dad', almost as if to mock me and to underline her closeness to him. Behind my back she sneered at my taste in clothes ('Palu's like a golliwog dressed in coloured rags. She thinks she knows English better than

I do and I was brought up with it!'), and I saw her victorious smile whenever Emo broke off his monologue of silence at dinner to talk to her.

I can smell from here the rotting entrails on the parquet floor. You visit the stinking room to see if your future has changed. Perhaps as they rot and bloat your future will change.

Love, let's talk about love. That phantom walking through the corridors or sitting silently at the dinner table is a man I love. Did I end up hating him or loving him? I gave him the benefit of the doubt because I thought he had become unbalanced and that his immersion into his world of darkness was not deliberate but a sign of defeat. I was yet to understand how willingly he had accepted the mantle of the Emperor of Darkness. See that dwarf moping in her giant bed. That is Palu and she doesn't know what to do. She wants his love again. She wants to be swallowed up by his love but she doesn't know how to stop being swallowed up by his darkness. She lies in bed all day reading her favourite novels and poems (Dickens, Lawson) in the hope that she will feel less lonely. She reads and reads, shutting out the country and western music, eating chocolates, masturbating to stop the heat which only he can satisfy. And inside her is a womb so empty that only the universe could fill it. Mr Gecko, you should have seen that love-starved, distraught woman growing plump in her silk sheets as if she were a black caterpillar in its cocoon. I felt paralysed and empty.

Mr Gecko, what is it, are you in pain? Are you ill? I saw my gecko writhing on the wall, his head twisting and turning as if it were cracking open. The nose began to fall off and the eyes move from their sockets, and from out of this mess of skin came a new head and brighter eyes. He wriggled his way free of the old skin and it dropped to the floor, leaving him translucent and shiny new. So gossamer thin is his new skin that the heart, beating quickly with exertion, looks as if it has no covering at all. Mr Stumpy, you are so beautiful. If only I could shed my sweaty, sickly skin and become new like you.

Emo, get out of my head!

You are dreaming of me, wanting me dead. I can feel your desire, your shivering hate inside me. My whole body is shivering with your bitterness. Larenkeni has told you of my refusal to sign the confession. He has come to your sick bed and inflamed you against me even more. In your restless sleep your dreams of revenge are terrible. Get out of my head!

I try to vomit you up but only blood comes from my mouth. It is said that a husband often has sympathy pains to match those of his pregnant wife: I am making you pregnant with my illness, Emo.

If only this illness were not so bad and I could sleep and dream you to death. Your dreamstone is sweating and bleeding like me.

I try to stand and shake Emo from my body.

Mr Gecko — run! Run! Flee this place of death.

If I do not survive, at least I want the forgiveness of the birds of paradise.

It is taking me hours to write these single sentences and I am finding concentration impossible. I must hide these notes.

I thought I hid them but this morning when I took away the brick in the wall, behind the dreamstone, they were gone. I panicked, wondering if they had been discovered. Perhaps I had imagined I hid them last night and in fact a guard had come in and found them on my bed as I slept. Everything

205

is so confused. I dreamt wild dreams. I turned into an insect and I flew through the palace and found you sleeping. Like a mosquito I drew blood from your arm and in return I gave you my foul blood. I had another dream in which I came into your room as Jayne serenaded you. I moved past her and found that she was singing to a stone President Emoti; you and the dreamstone had become one.

This illness is draining me. I feel like I'm floating. My breasts have shrunk and my ribs are showing through. It is as if the skeleton of death were pushing its way to the surface.

Dear bright, new gecko, sing to me. Let me feel your pulsating heart singing to me — drown out that wretched girl.

Perhaps I did dream that my manuscript had been stolen because an hour or so after a sleep (but how long did I sleep?) I took the brick away and found my manuscript again.

I want to write but find it hard to summon up the energy. My gecko is going *tsk, tsk* with concern and is moving down the wall towards my bed as if to make sure I can finish this thing. He is staring at me with his beautiful black, shiny eyes and he tilts his head to one side as if to peer under my skin to get a better idea of my condition. Don't bother, there is nothing under the skin, just bone. He laughs hoarsely at my joke. Our sense of humour is silly and we laugh like drunks. I will tell you a story, Mr Gecko, it's about me growing fat in the palace. Look at the weight Palu has put on! My dresses split as I walk and I feel as heavy as a dozen sacks of coffee beans. My maid buys me all the chocolates and coconut ice I want. Caye is a Highlander and one day while we were talking she told me of rumours her boyfriend had heard. It was said that the Highlands themselves had gone mad. I looked up from the bag of fat which encased me and asked what she meant by mad?

'It is said that the jungle has gone mad and that it's so fertile it's exploding with ripeness.'

I laughed loudly at her foolish story. Caye was offended, yet she went on, trying to convince me that the rumours were true. She told me that trees had grown ten times their normal height and fruit was so heavy that it took four men just to carry one pandanus fruit.

I had to hide these pages quickly, stuffing them under my mattress when I heard Nambweapa'w's footsteps coming down the corridor. He brought me a glass of water and some pills. He lifted up my head and made me drink the water and swallow the pills. Unusually kind, he treated me with almost a lover's tenderness. The doctor has apparently returned to the capital and Nambweapa'w had to steal the pills — or so he tells me.

'Why are you doing this for me?'

'I want you to live.'

I found the dramatic change in his attitude bewildering. He lay my head down on the sweat-ingrained pillow. I smelt no alcohol on his breath or spicy bark. It was as if he no longer needed courage to touch me. He wiped my brow with his handkerchief.

'You must live. I have heard that Larenkeni is coming back.'

The news did not surprise me. Undoubtedly Emo has instructed him to kill me. I am too ill to worry about my death. Nambweapa'w soaked his handkerchief in a mug of water and pressed it against my dry, blood encrusted lips. Out of the corner of my eye I saw the dreamstone move.

I blinked and saw it was still and I had imagined it I grabbed Nambweapa'w's arm. He momentarily flinched at the touch of a witch but then looked me straight in the eye as if he no longer feared me.

'I want to know...' I said and realised he couldn't hear me. He leaned forward to catch my voice. 'I want to know if the President is sick or not. Have you heard anything?'

'One of the fellows in the mess said that he had heard that the President was dying.'

A sort of happiness flooded through my veins. My dream-stone is working — I am destroying him!

Nambweapa'w left and my gecko came down the wall to inspect me like a doctor. He is near my face now as I write. His black marble eyes peer over my shoulder and he watches each word being written. So much effort does it take to hold the pencil that each word is like chiselling it onto stone.

Caye's stories of what was happening in the Highlands disturbed me and I asked Emo if he knew of them. I got no answer from him. A darkness deep as night had gripped him. The angels were not enough and he sought the comfort of a peasant soothsayer who read the future in the entrails of freshly killed pigs.

I found out, though, that Colonel Akwanaamae's troops had been fighting some sort of rebellion in the Highlands for months. The war was secret but there were stories that there had been much bloodshed. Colonel Akwanaamae's animosity towards other tribal groups had become legendary.

I knew that my request to visit the Highlands would never be agreed to so I decided to go there secretly while Emo and Jayne toured the Night People's territories, being greeted as physical manifestations of Sido and his daughter. Once they had flown out I took a car from the increasingly large Presidential car pool (it had multiplied so that Emo's double had his own cars to fool would-be assassins) and I headed off on the one road that had been built into the Highlands. Emo had once had a vision of the whole country being united by a network of roads but during the years of his Presidency only a dirt road had been built into the Highlands. You ask, Mr Gecko, why I undertook this journey. Deep down, I suppose, I was still a Highlander and the Highlands were still my home. We never forget or forgive where we were born. I also think that I wanted to seek just one more confirmation of my husband's reign of darkness and so, learn to hate him. Picture me, Mr Gecko, there I am, plump as a breastfed suckling, sitting on three silk pillows, heading off into the darkness in my air-conditioned Mercedes Benz.

I am finding it harder to breathe. Give me strength. I drifted off for a while and dreamt I was at your bedside. You had turned into a bat demon and your mouth was open. I looked into it and saw it was shining. I put my fingers down it and felt that your teeth were golden. I heard a death rattle from deep inside your throat. I was scared because I felt as though I were inside the bat demon's cave and that the bat demon was about to swallow me. In the middle of this dream I thought I awoke and saw Nambweapa'w standing next to my bed, staring at me, pity in his eyes.

Yet when I did wake up a guard came in and asked when I had last seen Nambweapa'w. I said I didn't remember, nor did I care. It seems as though he has run away.

I do not think I am long for this world, Mr Gecko. When I cough, blood comes from my mouth and there is pus seeping from my cunt. I can hear the ghosts outside my cell hungrily waiting for my liver. But I must tell you, dear handsome gecko, of my journey.

The first village I stopped at in the Highlands was empty. It smelt of slow death. At the rear of the village was a pile of corpses. The only survivor of a massacre, a hunchback, was trying to bury them so that they would be able to journey into the afterlife among the Sky People. Colonel Akwanaa-mae's soldiers had killed everyone, including women and children. The hunchback had escaped and hidden in the jungle for two days. The soldiers had also desecrated the menstrual hut by throwing men's bodies into it and had pissed and shat on the sacred objects in the spirit house. I knew the hunchback would die before he could finish his task — the desecration and murder had destroyed his soul.

I was too ashamed to say who I was and I drove on, finding that the slaughter had continued deep into the Highlands. The troops had even bayoneted pregnant women because they had 'dissidents' in their wombs. Wild animals ate the bodies that were left to rot, unburied, in the bush. As if to mock the dead, the soldiers did not kill the diseased and the ill. These unfortunates were left deliberately as the last members of famous tribes. Trying to maintain the food gardens these survivors worked from dawn to dusk to provide for themselves, moving like crabs along the hillsides.

As I grew closer to my birthplace the silence became more oppressive. It was as if every living thing had vanished; there were no insects and no birds sung. I came upon a village where I found the surviving women hiding in the menstrual hut. Their newly born children were all deformed. Some had arms like flippers, others were blind and some had so many fingers that their hands were useless. It was a terrible sight, Mr Gecko. I cursed Emo's name and that of Colonel Akwanaamae. Fearing that the same thing had happened to my village I drove on until the road faded away and I walked the last few kilometres. As I walked I heard planes overhead, droning endlessly as if inspecting each village from the air. Nearing my village I became aware of just how big everything was. Trees thrust themselves into the sky like giants and vines were the thickness of a man's body. The smell of the jungle was a horrific mixture of overrich fertility and putrefaction.

My village was empty, as if it had been so for some time. It had changed little since I was a child. The only thing missing was my parents' house which had been burnt down after my father's murders to get rid of the evil. The dreamstones of the spirit house were scattered on the ground. Without the dreamstones the tribe would wander the earth for eternity, unable to seek rest or shelter. I saw empty bullet shells covering the ground and imagined what had happened to everyone. Before leaving I visited the garden. Rounding the chief's hut I was astonished by what I saw. Bananas were thick as a man's arm, taro plants were twice their normal size and sugar cane grew as high as trees. Everything was monstrously huge, even the bougainvillaea that wound its way up the cane and into the enormous trees had flowers the size of plates. I did not know if what I saw was real or if I were hallucinating. As I stood there remembering Caye's words, bananas split open and sugar cane stems cracked along their sides as if ruptured by an axe, the sugary juice gushing down the trunk like monsoonal rain. It seemed as though the garden were growing before my eyes, afflicted by an unholy ripeness, and once the plants reached the limit of their rampant growth they exploded with overripeness.

Terrified, I ran from the garden believing, like Caye, that the Highlands had become the territory of the demons who had escaped from the Golden Mountain. Unable to get back to Port Andrews that night I drove down into the valley, following the coffee truck trail, the one that had once brought me to Mister Bacon's plantation.

Approaching the plantation I thought the house had vanished but when I got closer I realised that it was hidden behind coffee bushes so massive that they were like trees. When I reached the house I saw that it was run down and empty. It looked as though no one had lived in it for a year or more. Once I thought it was a palace but really it was quite a small place, and the hut where Maz and I had once slept was the size of an outhouse. I visited Mister Bacon's grave. It took me some time because I went the long way for fear of being splashed with the unnatural juice of the exploding coffee berries which were the size of apples.

Mister Bacon's grave was covered in river reeds. It seemed centuries ago that I had rolled on the freshly turned earth in an agony of mourning. Look at me now, I said to him, your little thin girl has turned into a terrified fat woman. I listened intently for his reply but all I could hear was the sporadic noise of the coffee berries exploding like firecrackers at the completion of their grotesque cycle of fertility. I did not know what to do, I felt lost and alone. I fell to my knees and called out to Mister Bacon to help me but my pleas went unanswered. I stayed with him until nightfall and then, scared of what the night might bring, I returned to the house. I tried to sleep but my dreams were full of my dead tribesmen forever wandering the limbo between death and the afterlife. In the morning I saw that my car, which I had parked near a boundary of coffee bushes, was splattered with red, rotten-smelling juice. 'Run, run away from here, Palu — this place is evil. Run!' I heard Mister Bacon shout from the river. I rushed to the car just as a plane, emitting green vapour, flew low over the plantation.

By the time I got back to Port Andrews, the car splotched with red juice and sprayed with a green mist, I had realised that Colonel Akwanaamae's troops had been using some sort of monstrous defoliant. I confronted Emo with what I had seen and he did not deny it. He told me, as if he were a scientist conducting an experiment, that the defoliant (newly developed in America from a chemical used in the Vietnam war) eradicated a jungle by making it monstrously ripe.

'But why are you doing this,' I asked.

'Because the opposition hides out in the jungle. Soon they will have no place to hide.'

I told him of the bodies and empty villages I had seen but he did not seem to care. He stood like a carved statue in the middle of the reception room, oblivious to my anger. It was like talking to a stranger. Darkness had finally consumed him like a black fire and his world was now evil. His deformed fingers had created the deformed children, and his unnatural mind had concocted an unnatural world of nature which destroyed itself by its own fertility.

I told him that what he was doing was wrong and I tried to remind him of what he had wanted to achieve when he first became President, but he did not listen. 'I am not going to be caught up in your darkness anymore, Emo.'

He mused on this in silence for a while. 'What are you going to do? I hope nothing foolish.'

I had no idea of what my next move was. Does a wife ever betray her husband, no matter what evil things he has done?

'I have put up with you for a long time, Palu. Not many

men would still be married to a woman with a dead cunt. Or a witch.'

I laughed. 'A witch!'

'I know your wiles. You have taken all my seed and made me impotent. You are a witch.' I realised that in believing I was a witch he feared me.

Jayne suddenly came into the reception room and smiled at me. 'You should take off weight, Palu. You look like a medicine ball.'

I didn't feel like an argument and was about to leave when there was a smashing sound overhead. I looked up and saw a bat come crashing in through the skylight, sending broken glass tumbling down on us. Jayne ran into a corner, screaming. The bat fell slowly and then began to fly around the room in clumsy circles. Jayne moaned, frightened out of her wits. Emo had not moved and pieces of glass had landed on his shoulders and hair. He watched the bat flying beneath the dull grey ceiling, astonished by its presence. The bat filled the room with a musky, unclean odour and made no move to escape. Emo looked at me and I realised he knew what I was thinking *this bat has come home to the cave of the bat demon!*

I hear you now on the radio and your voice is high-pitched. Soon only bats will hear you. So high is your strained voice that I cannot understand what you are saying. The palace will soon be filled with thousands of bats coming home to roost on the ceiling above your sick bed.

I gave my account of the slaughter in the Highlands to a foreign reporter whose report was published in the main newspapers overseas.

'You have betrayed me,' was all Emo said when he found

214

out. I didn't betray Emo — I betrayed that bat demon, President Emoti.

Your voice sounds scared, Jayne. Tonight you sing as if you know what is about to befall you.

Caye said that she had seen President Emoti go into his angel room the morning after he had written a press release saying that Mrs President was ill and crazy with childlessness, and that she suffered from Highland chauvinism. When I was told he had vanished into the angel room I knew my time was up. I put on my best dress and waited in the reception room for Larenkeni to arrest me. He was unnerved by my calmness. I was smiling because I knew you were shivering in fear at the feet of your blood bespattered angels. 'You are going to Kunugamamae,' he said. I had never heard of it but knew by the length of the name that it was somewhere in the Night People's territory. I did not know that this place existed. I did not know that your darkness was as profound as this.

I woke this morning, thinking I had woken into a dream. Bird of paradise feathers covered me and the cell floor. They were blue, green, red, yellow, black and orange. Astonished guards came to gaze at this extraordinary sight and the governor was sent for. He demanded to know how the feathers had got in here. 'I do not know,' I replied. I saw it in his eyes, and in the eyes of the guards *she is a witch! The stories are true, she is a witch!* I felt gloriously happy because I *did* know how the feathers had gotten in here; the birds of paradise have forgiven me! It is their sign of forgiveness. My heart felt as light as a cloud. I wanted to cry out 'Ripperty Kye A-hoo!' Even when the guards came

215

in and swept up the feathers into hessian bags I still felt a sense of rapture. They took the feathers out into the compound and burnt them.

Now the whole prison must know of the miracle. First the fireflies and now the feathers — what more proof do they need that I am a witch? I don't care. I have been forgiven. My gecko is running up and down the walls like a dervish, his heart thumping out, joyously, *Ripperty Kye A-hoo! Ripperty Kye A-hoo!*

This morning I slept as peacefully as I had in a long time but I woke up with pus seeping from between my legs. The pain is unbearable. My stomach is torn to pieces.

Nambweapa'w has returned after his mysterious disappearance. He had a curious smile on his face. If you're going to execute me, do it now, I thought, but he did nothing of the sort. Instead he gently wiped the pus away and cleaned my vagina with disinfectant. He gave me some water to drink but I could not keep it down. I asked him why he was helping me.

'Because I poisoned you,' he said simply.

I thought he was teasing me. 'Why poison me and then try to help me?'

'I thought you were a witch. I don't anymore. I poisoned your meals. You're a hard woman to kill — it was enough poison to finish off a platoon.'

He held me tightly and tenderly like a lover. I was stunned by his admission but gradually I understood; I had not dreamt that these pages had been stolen. Nambweapa'w had found them and read what I had written. It was he who had gone into the jungle to get the bird of paradise feathers in the hope that I would believe I had been forgiven.

'I hate you for doing that,' I told him.

'I poisoned you because I thought you had enchanted me.'

'I'm not talking about the poison — I will die anyway — I hate you for the feathers. I thought the birds of paradise had truly forgiven me for what I did to them.'

I tried to push myself free of him, feeling full of despair, but I am as weak as a child and he held me in his grip. I threatened to tell the governor about what he had done but he knew I wouldn't.

'Will you tell Larenkeni about what I've written,' I asked, he promised he wouldn't and I felt calm for the first time in days. I slept in his arms, occasionally waking when the pain got too much.

I dreamt of you, Emo. I saw myself lying next to you in your sick bed. Your eyes were black, like a bat's, and you could not talk but only emit high-pitched sounds. From a distant room I heard Jayne crying in fear — she can already feel the knives and spears of a bloody death.

Lying in your bed you want to call out for water, not because you are thirsty, but because you want someone to come. There is a fear growing in your brain like some deadly night flower: flunkies and aides are the very people who will first sense your overthrow. So where are they now? There is an oppressive silence throughout the palace. Have they fled? If you had the strength you would crawl to the angel room and die amidst the comfort of angels. Do not dream, you tell yourself — dreams are full of Palu and she is violently attacking you.

Your body is writhing and twisting in pain. The thought whirls through your mind again and again that the nation is like your body — it, too, is going to rack and ruin; once you die, the nation will die. You have no willpower to survive and neither does the nation. I hear you, Emo. I feel your shivering, racked body. My words *you are the bat demon* are haunting you. Look, your dreamstone is quaking too at

217

the thought of your bedroom filled with squealing bats.

I woke up to find Nambweapa'w cleaning my arse. Apparently I had shat myself while I was sleeping.

'Will you forgive me for poisoning you?' he asked as he soaped me. I saw his young, bewildered face. It was like the faces of those tribesmen in their arse grass visiting Port Andrews for the first time, standing in awe before motor cars and electric street lights. I could not forgive him, the pain is too great.

The effort of writing these lines is taxing me greatly. I feel exhausted after each word. While I was resting, recovering from what I had written, I closed my eyes. After a few minutes I felt something crawling through my hair and down my forehead. I was too exhausted to be frightened. It came to rest on one of my eyelids. I felt its beating heart. It was my gecko, thinking I might be near death, trying to give me life with the heat of his own heart. He sat on my eyelid for sometime, his soft, velvety body as gentle as a lover's kiss. I thanked him for what he had done. He grinned. I take back all my thoughts about you being a coward, Mr Gecko.

The pig's entrails lie rotting on the palace floor, flies and small animals are feeding on the evil-smelling mess. The soothsayer has fled. Your future is all used up.

I am not writing anymore Nambweapa'w is doing it for me he is writing down what I say I am too exhausted and too ill to write anymore Larenkeni visited me hoping I was dead but I smiled at him and said he would have to kill me himself he did not like my confidence and he asked me if I would sign the confession this time but I told him to go take a jump.

I dreamt of you and you were being blown by my wind through the corridors of the palace blowing away like a piece of tissue paper.

Nambweapa'w do your ears hear what I hear on the radio do you hear what is on the radio it is the high-pitched cry of a bat demon I must defeat him and I will what has happened is that his vision is a vision full of darkness and it is ripe monstrously ripe and it is going to explode and crack open and there will be nothing inside it just a hollow shell and the darkness will be blown away by the wind of my dream.

Guards are whistling outside my window and they are whistling like flunkies of the bat demon coming to execute someone and I am not scared oh no I am not frightened because I know that it is they who are scared because they think I am a witch and I do I really do forgive you Namb-weapa'w because you have given me immortality everyone believes I am a witch and I know the stories about the fireflies and the bird of paradise feathers have got back to Emo and he is stunned because he only half believed I was a witch and now he knows I am going to become immortal an immortal myth of President Emoti's wife as witch and I will join you Emo in the land of legends if you are not destroyed by then and in the land of legends I will seek you out and destroy you and if you are not already dead people will talk about my witch's power when they ransack the palace dreams of your immortality will vanish and they will carve open your body on the palace steps and shout out to the sky *he is mortal he is not Sido* and outside my window hear them Nambweapa'w they are yelling out how they are going to kill the witch this pain is so intense I wish I was a changeling is this how you poison witches in the backblocks?

Once I loved Emo and he loved me when he lay on the bed he looked like a glistening black starfish wet with the sweat of passion and oh how beautiful he looked once I loved you Emo and still I can remember your sweet smell on my skin and the way you danced and made love on independence night but that was another person once there was a boy who came out of the marsh fog and his prospects were good and I asked Mister Bacon if he had had a life like David Copperfield and he laughed telling me Australia wasn't England I was just out of the jungle you see and not unlike you Nambweapa'w but at least you had some education and Emo is dying oh I can feel it right down deep in my marrow can't you hear the nervous footsteps in the corridors and the shouting in the compound?

There is no more Jayne on the radio and no more speeches the silence is terrifying the guards.

Where were you Nambweapa'w I woke up and found the most horrible thing had happened there was a bloody blot on the wall and blowflies buzzing around it and when I looked closer I saw that it was my Mr Gecko he is dead he is dead some guard with Larenkeni's help must have done it he is dead my friend is dead the string is broken the string is broken broken.

I cannot believe my friend is dead I know what it means I am to die soon when I saw my gecko my sweet sweet gecko was dead Larenkeni came in and demanded I sign the confession I said I would never sign it because it was full of lies and even if I signed it I would still be executed he said Mrs Emoti I will have your body chopped up into pieces and cast all over the compound well I had to laugh because that is what a chief once did to his wife and he threw her butchered body out the back and her limbs grew into a garden and my limbs will grow and the prison will become a garden again the jungle will take back this barren island and fill it with life and birds of paradise and you Emo will die in your cave in a world of lonely darkness and if you are not dead by the time I am then I will hunt you down through the afterlife I know you can hear because look your dreamstone is splitting cracking open and I know you can hear me open your eyes look out your bedroom all the palace corridors are filled with the brilliant light of fireflies and even your angels have flown away mark my words I will search for you relentlessly and I will capture your soul and strangle it but I feel there will be no need for that because you will be dead soon and the barren defoliated world you created will grow once more and your vision of darkness will shrivel in the sunlight you are not Sido you are a man and a husband and your wife knows you better than anyone and it is my revenge to say that you pissed shat and shivered with fear and cried like any other man and you were weak enough to have allowed yourself to become the emperor of darkness.

I hear birds of paradise and they are calling out we forgive you Palu.

Thank you for cleaning me Nambweapa'w I hear the loudspeaker in the compound calling all the prisoners to hurry up so they can watch my execution and you must hurry and dress me how thin I've grown I have waited years to be forgiven by the birds of paradise Nambweapa'w oh how beautiful your smile is I would like to make love to you right now I am happy because I have been forgiven and because I have won I have beaten you Emo look Nambweapa'w look the dreamstone has cracked and crumbled into pieces the size of pebbles when I die Nambweapa'w throw them

into the well they are useless now Emo oh my beloved my
enemy my vision has conquered yours the emperor of darkness
is dead and poor Larenkeni knows that even if he cuts me
up into a thousand pieces I will not die you have given me
immortality Nambweapa'w I am going to join Mister Bacon
by the side of the river and there we will live for eternity
and I am so happy so happy I cannot stop from crying out
for joy my cry is filling the whole of the prison and I am
yelling out *Ripperty Kye A-hoo!* sing exultantly *Ripperty
Kye A-hoo! Ripperty Kye A-hoo!*